**"I'm working on s[omething that]
concerns the Cha[tsfields,]** Sophie said finally.

"Clearly not something they would be very happy about."

"Well, probably not. But I can see you're not one of their fans. It would please you to know that I'm not a big fan of the Chatsfield family either. And I don't think they necessarily deserve the somewhat pristine public reputation they seem to have cultivated recently."

"So what is it you're after?" asked Sheikh Zayn Al-Ahmar.

"A scandal."

"Of course, I should've known you were after a scandal. What good reporter isn't?" Unfortunately, she was very close to a scandal. One that would involve his family, his sister. One that was simply unacceptable to have out in the open.

"Well, exactly."

"And you know that I'm not James's biggest fan?"

"Well, clearly not. As he seems to have gotten himself involved with your sister."

And just like that he realized that whatever else she knew, she knew too much. With an entire newspaper to back her, she would be relaying this information to interested parties, who would likely do much more digging than he would want done.

"Yes indeed." And just like that, he realized he had made his decision. He leaned forward and pressed the intercom button on the partition between the backseat and the front seat. "We are not going back to the hotel. We will be going straight to the airport."

The world's most elite hotel is looking for a jewel in its crown and Spencer Chatsfield has found it. But Isabella Harrington, the girl from his past, refuses to sell!

Now the world's most decadent destinations have become a chessboard in this game of power, passion and pleasure...

Welcome to

The Chatsfield

Synonymous with style, sensation...and scandal!

With the eight Chatsfield siblings happily married and settling down, it's time for a new generation of Chatsfields to shine!

Spencer Chatsfield steps in as CEO, determined to prove his worth. But when he approaches Isabella Harrington, of Harringtons Boutique Hotels, with the offer of a merger that would benefit them both...he's left with a stinging red palm-shaped mark on his cheek!

And so begins a game of cat and mouse that will shape the future of the Chatsfields and the Harringtons forever.

But neither knows that there's one stakeholder with the power to decide their fate...and their identity will shock both the Harringtons *and* the Chatsfields.

Just who will come out on top?

Find out in

Eight titles to collect—you won't want to miss out!

Sheikh's Desert Duty

—

Maisey Yates

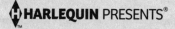
HARLEQUIN PRESENTS®

Special thanks and acknowledgment are given to Maisey Yates for her contribution to The Chatsfield series.

ISBN-13: 978-0-373-13780-0

Sheikh's Desert Duty

First North American publication 2015

Copyright © 2015 by Harlequin Books S.A.

Recycling programs for this product may not exist in your area.

Printed in U.S.A.

www.Harlequin.com

USA TODAY bestselling author **MAISEY YATES** lives in rural Oregon with her three children and her husband, whose chiseled jaw and arresting features continue to make her swoon. She feels the epic trek she takes several times a day from her office to her coffeemaker is a true example of her pioneer spirit.

In 2009, at the age of twenty-three, Maisey sold her first book. Since then it's been a whirlwind of sexy alpha males and happily-ever-afters, and she wouldn't have it any other way. Maisey divides her writing time between dark, passionate category romances set just about everywhere on earth and light, sexy contemporary romances set practically in her backyard. She believes that she clearly has the best job in the world.

Other titles by Maisey Yates available in ebook:

TO DEFY A SHEIKH
ONE NIGHT TO RISK IT ALL
PRETENDER TO THE THRONE
(The Call of Duty)
FORGED IN THE DESERT HEAT

To Pippa, Laura and Jackie.
Thanks for talking me through this one.
Sometimes you need the whole team.

CHAPTER ONE

SHEIKH ZAYN AL-AHMAR had many regrets in his life. The kind of regrets that reached into the darkness in the middle of the night, and tried to strangle him while he slept. The kind of regrets that followed him all through the day, and informed his every action; constant reminders of why he'd had to leave the old version of himself behind, and become something entirely different.

But however pressing his past regrets might be, right now he could think of only one. Right now, his most sincere regret was that he could not close his fist around James Chatsfield's throat and end the worthless man's life here and now, in an alley behind his family hotel.

Instead, he settled for something much less satisfying. He curled his hands around the lapels of James's jacket and shoved the other man back against the brick wall. It was a violent action but, Zayn found, not quite violent enough for his current mood.

"I'm not quite sure what has your knickers in a twist, Al-Ahmar," James said. His pretty-boy face, filled with that kind of insouciance he excelled at, only enraged Zayn further. The mocking gleam in his eyes only stoking the fires higher. Because Zayn was so well acquainted with both. Because Zayn might well have been looking into a mirror that showed a reflection of the past.

But most especially because what the man had done was unforgivable.

"I think you very well know, Chatsfield." Zayn didn't see the point in playing games. Not here in a darkened alley with no one around to witness his actions.

For sixteen years, his life had been consumed with the protection of his family. With the protection of his reputation, and that of his country. And now, this one man was threatening to undo it all. Right now, this man represented the single greatest threat to Surhaadi, its people and to everything Zayn had built his new life on.

"Please, tell me this isn't about your sister."

Violence surged through Zayn's blood, and he took the opportunity to reacquaint the back of James's head with the wall. "What else could this be about? You have dishonored her. And in so doing you have dishonored me, the royal family and my people."

James didn't even have the decency to look scared. Instead of trembling, he arched a brow, his lips curved into a mocking smile. "That is a very heavy burden to place on one woman's body. I was not aware that the integrity of the nation rested upon your sister's maidenhead."

"You have no place to comment on integrity," Zayn said, tightening his grasp on James. "You are a man in possession of none."

"But at least I don't treat women like they are my property."

No, James Chatsfield would never treat a woman like she was his property. Because once he had slept with a woman, he had no further association with her. Worse than treating them like he owned them, he treated them as though they were disposable. Paper dolls that he could dress, and undress, at will, before crumpling them up and throwing them away.

And in Zayn's sister's case, leaving them forever altered. Leaving her with child. A fact Zayn preferred James Chatsfield never even know. He didn't have a right to know. Because he had never had a right to touch Leila in the first place. And as far as Zayn was concerned, James would never touch her again.

"Perhaps not, Chatsfield, but the fact remains

that you have badly handled what belongs to me. My family, anyone beneath my protection, belongs to me. You are fortunate we are *not* in my country, for there, I would not hesitate to remove the member that committed the offense."

Chatsfield shifted, suddenly breaking Zayn's hold, his agility and strength surprising. Indeed, contrary to Zayn's initial appraisal, the man was not the lazy playboy he appeared to be. Oh, the fact remained that he was a playboy, but there was a sharpness to him that Zayn found surprising.

"You're positively biblical, Al-Ahmar." Chatsfield straightened his suit jacket, and his tie, brushing off an imagined bit of dust. "Sadly, I haven't the time to engage in any eye-for-an-eye nonsense."

Rage poured through Zayn, and he wanted nothing more than to wipe the smirk off Chatsfield's face. But he would not risk drawing attention. Would not risk giving Chatsfield a reason to wonder if there was more to Zayn's rage than him simply sleeping with Leila. "You will not speak of your dalliance with my sister to anyone in the press."

James made a scoffing sound. "Why would I ever speak to the press about such a thing?"

"Because while Leila was simply one in a long line of your exploits, the fact remains she is a princess. The media would love to get their hands on that."

"You insult me, Al-Ahmar. In this country I am royalty in my own right. I hardly need to trade on your name to create a scandal so I can get featured in the headlines. I have my own."

"If you breathe a word of this to anyone, I will have your head. And I do not speak metaphorically."

Something in Chatsfield's expression hardened. "Oh, I have no doubt." He straightened his jacket yet again and turned, walking back inside the hotel, leaving Zayn alone in the alleyway to curse into the emptiness around him.

The feeling of helplessness that was pouring through him was unwelcome, and all too familiar. It echoed a time he'd failed another sister. Another time the problems had been too big to fix. Regret piling on top of regret.

Rain was starting to fall, the only light coming from a lone streetlamp, casting everything in a yellow glow. Zayn's mind was racing, his pulse in overdrive. If any of this got out, the press would have a field day. He had no idea what Leila intended to do about her pregnancy, and with the heightened interest surrounding the royal family, due to Zayn's own upcoming marriage, she was in a much more precarious position than she might have been.

She was vulnerable enough without introducing the variable of public opinion and scrutiny. That would add pressure she didn't need, judgment she didn't deserve. No, he would not have that. He would not expose his family to such criticism and judgment. Not again. Not while he drew breath.

He heard a clattering sound in the corner of the alley, a trash can turning over on its side, a blur of motion catching his eye.

He was not alone. And he and Chatsfield had not been the only two involved in the conversation that had taken place only minutes before. They had a witness.

And that was unacceptable.

The feeling of helplessness drained, a shot of adrenaline moving through his veins. Action. He craved action. He craved a plan.

Zayn stalked toward the movement, his body on high alert, muscles tensing, ready to strike. When a man lived as he did, he had ample time to train his body. And Zayn had done just that. Had taken every opportunity to spend hours channeling physical frustration into strength training.

He didn't fear whatever would be waiting for him in the shadow. He had no reason to. Because he had no doubt whatsoever that he was the most dangerous thing in this alley.

There was more clattering, followed by a squeak, and he acted, reaching into the darkness and coming up with a fistful of hair, resistance and a sharp squeal.

Not the sound of a hardened criminal.

He released his hold on the person he had seized, and straightened.

"Who are you?" he asked. "What do you want?"

"Ow," his quarry made a plaintive noise.

"I doubt very much that you're injured," he said. "Come into the light."

The intruder obliged, moving from the shadow and into the golden haze cast by the streetlight. He wasn't entirely certain what he'd expected, but the slim blonde with long honey-colored hair, disheveled—likely from when he had grabbed it—wearing a sequined dress with a hemline that fell well above her knee, and mutinous expression on her face, was not at all what he'd imagined he might find.

"I am very much injured." She sniffed.

He crossed his arms over his chest. "If you are so easily damaged, it is advisable that perhaps you shouldn't spend time hiding in dark alleys. They are dangerous."

"It would seem so." She was frantically straightening her dress now, moving her hands over her slight curves, smoothing the wrinkles in the fabric.

"What are you doing here?" he asked, suspicion pressing down on him.

"I followed Chatsfield out into the alley." She straightened, flipping long hair back over her shoulder, a pale, glimmering wave in the streetlight.

That made sense. She was very likely one of Chatsfield's hopefuls, or one of his previous acquisitions. Probably trying to find out if she could finagle another night in his bed. Or perhaps just hoping she could trade on her connection with him for money or status.

Either way, she was dangerous. Either way, she would have motive to take her story to the press. The opportunity for revenge in the hands of a woman scorned by a playboy could prove dangerous for his sister.

"I see. And how much did you hear?"

Her eyes, which were already quite wide, widened further. "Nothing of interest. I was actually quite bored. I was *actually* taking a nap."

"Try again." He found he had little patience to continue standing out here as rain began to pour down on them. He found he had little patience for any of this. To face another failure where his family was concerned. To face another threat to them, after all they had been through.

It was in his power to spare them more pain, and he would do so. And he would not let one large-eyed blonde get in his way.

"I'm really into the free-food movement. And I like to make sure that there are no salvageable edibles in various trash cans surrounding posh hotels." She started to move away from him. "You would be surprised how much gourmet food is simply tossed. I have found foie gras that was still quite fresh just cast out into the gutter. It's egregious."

"You said you followed Chatsfield out into the alley."

She squinted. "I thought he might be looking for the foie gras."

"It is getting quite cold out." He reached out and grabbed hold of her arm, and she tugged back. But he held fast. "Why don't we finish this conversation in my car?"

"Oh, you know—" she waved a hand "—I would, but I have a thing."

"What thing?" he asked.

"A thing that is not getting into a car with a stranger."

"I feel that after all you must have surely heard from your vantage point, we can hardly be considered strangers."

He tugged her along through the alley with him, heading to where his limousine was idling.

She walked along with him, but her hesitance was clear. For a moment he questioned himself. Asked himself what the hell he was doing.

But then he imagined Leila, in her distress, confessing her indiscretion, and worrying about the consequences. No, he would do whatever he had to do. No matter what that was.

There was no room, no time, for guilt.

"I really need to go," she said. "My bicycle is double-parked. I think there's a timer on the rack. I bet they're going to cut my chain."

"I will buy you a new bicycle."

"That one has sentimental value."

He paused, and looked down at her. "Why did you ride a bicycle in this weather? In that dress."

"We don't all hemorrhage gold."

"No, indeed we do not. I imagine you have realized that James Chatsfield does."

"What exactly are you implying?"

He propelled her forward to the passenger door of the limousine, and jerked it open. "I'm implying that you need to get into my car now."

"I don't think I will."

"I'm sorry, I see you've confused my command with a request." Not breaking his hold on her, he moved down into the limo, bringing her with him, her soft body flush against his.

And because it had been so very long since he had touched a woman, even given the circumstances, he could not help but take a moment to pause and enjoy the feel of her against him.

She wiggled, her bottom coming into contact with things he would rather not have her in contact with. "What are you doing?" she shrieked.

He did not answer. He only held fast to her, trying to figure out exactly where to take it from here.

Though he was immediately drawn back to the moment by the feel of her body against his.

It was in moments like this, moments when heat and curves overtook the gravity of the situation, that he wondered whether or not he'd truly managed to change. Or if he had simply spent years burying his weakness beneath the rock of good intention. Though, as he had so rarely found himself in this position since he had changed the focus of his life, he supposed it was neither here nor there. It did not matter how soft this woman was. It did not matter how good it felt to have her in his arms.

All that mattered was Leila. Her honor. Her safety, both physical and emotional.

No one could be allowed to compromise that.

He closed the limo door, and kept his hold on the woman, who seemed to have gone limp in his grasp. For one moment he wondered if she had fainted. And then she started talking again.

"Somehow I don't think you've brought me in here because you're concerned about me getting wet." She turned to face him, concern lighting her eyes.

"It's quite possible you're correct."

"Are you kidnapping me?"

"I feel that term implies both premeditation and a desire for ransom money. And as we've established that I hemorrhage gold, and you do not, I have no need of ransom money. Also, there was no premeditation involved, how could there have been? I had no idea you would be in the alleyway."

"I don't feel that either of those things is a necessary requirement to call something kidnapping." She cocked her head to the side. "Are you detaining me against my will?"

"That all depends." He shifted as the car started to move, releasing his hold on her. "Do you want to stay in the limo?"

"No."

"Then yes, I am detaining you against your will."

"Well, I think we're going to have a problem." She lifted her chin, her expression defiant, eyes glittering.

He looked around the darkened car, at the streetlights moving quickly by, bathing her face in quick flashes of light. "Excuse me, little *sheikha*, but I fail to see what problem you could possibly pose to me in this position."

She drew back slightly. "I scream very loudly."

"I am certain you do." He reached up and thumped his knuckles on the back of the black partition between the back and front seats. "But everything in here is soundproof. And bulletproof."

"What does it being bulletproof have to do with anything?"

"Just in case you were going to get some ideas about breaking a window. If a sniper's bullet couldn't manage it, you certainly can't." He leaned back in his seat. "I don't want you breaking an elbow trying to force your way out."

She sniffed loudly. "I don't know why you would worry about my elbow. Not when you have seized my person."

"I have not broken your person, have I?" She only glared at him, her expression mutinous. "No, I have not," he said, answering his own question. "And I would prefer to keep it that way."

"I assume this is supposed to make me feel calmer about the fact that you forced me into your car and are now taking me who knows where."

"I know where." A bit of an overstatement.

He wasn't entirely certain where he was going to take her, or what he was going to do with her. He didn't know if she knew who he was, or what she had overheard. And he needed to find a way to ascertain that without giving away any more than he needed to.

He only knew he had to keep her. That this was his chance to seize control of this situation. To fix it.

"Oh, how interesting," she said. "I might appreciate being let in on that information."

"Sorry, that sort of information is a privilege."

"What are you doing? Why are you bothering with me? I'm not anyone. No, scratch that, I am someone. I work for a very prestigious newspaper and if you don't let me go…"

"You're a reporter?"

"Yes," she said, seeming to change tactic abruptly. "I am. An intrepid one. A real one. Kind of a big deal."

"What were you doing in that alley?" He had to know now, because if she was telling the truth, that meant that she was far more dangerous to him than an ex-lover of Chatsfield's would be. She was the very thing he feared most. The very thing that could do the most damage to his family.

To Leila.

Leila had made a mistake in sleeping with

James. But ultimately, Leila was so innocent that her stake in it was much lower than Chatsfield's. She had been taken advantage of, of that Zayn was certain. And this woman would drag her before the press, who would tear her apart like ravenous wolves. Because she was a woman, because the media, and the public, would see her fault as the greater fault.

Because she was a princess and being royalty she would be the bigger target.

No, he could not allow it. He had already put one innocent sister in harm's way. He'd already failed her. In a way there was no coming back from. He would be damned if he'd do it again.

He would fix this. By any means necessary. A disgruntled lover might have taken a payoff, but not a reporter. No, this would require more extreme measures.

He would remove her from contact if need be. Even if he had to pick her up and carry her back to Surhaadi.

She hesitated, clearly trying to decide what she could say now that would help her out of her current situation. That was enough to inform him that whatever she said was very likely to be a lie.

"I was following James," she said finally. "I'm working on something that concerns the Chatsfield family."

"Clearly not something they would be very happy about."

"Well, probably not. But I can see you're not James's biggest fan. It would please you to know that I'm not a big fan of the Chatsfield family as a whole. And I don't think they necessarily deserve the somewhat pristine reputation in the public they seem to have cultivated recently."

"So what is it you're after?"

"A scandal."

"Of course, I should've known you were after a scandal. What good reporter isn't?" Unfortunately, she was very close to a scandal. One that would involve his family, his sister. One that was simply unacceptable to have out in the open.

"Well, exactly."

"And you know that I'm not James's biggest fan?"

"Well, clearly not. As he seems to have gotten himself involved with your sister."

Instantly he realized that whatever else she knew, she knew too much. With an entire newspaper to back her, she would be parlaying this information to interested parties, who would likely do much more digging than he would like done.

"Yes, indeed." And just like that, he made his decision. He leaned forward and pressed the intercom button on the partition between the backseat and the front seat. "We are not going back to the hotel. We will be going straight to the airport."

CHAPTER TWO

IT TOOK QUITE a bit to rattle Sophie Parsons. She hadn't gotten where she was in life by being a shrinking violet. But currently, she was feeling extremely rattled. And slightly like shrinking.

She figured it was understandable. As she had just been forced into a limo by a man who stood nearly a foot taller than she did, and who must outweigh her by more than one hundred pounds of lean muscle. And now they were going to the airport, apparently.

She eyed the speedily passing scenery and considered attempting doing a tuck and roll.

"The doors are locked."

It seemed he was a mind reader in addition to being a kidnapper. Except he seemed to take offense to the term *kidnapper*. Did she really care? She took offense to being forced inside of a limo and taken to God knows where.

"Right, well, it's not like I was going to go jumping out of a moving vehicle." Except she had been thinking of doing just that. "Although you've given me no reason to believe that I wouldn't be better off taking my chances with the asphalt than I am staying here with you."

"You have nothing to fear from me. I do not intend to hurt you."

She assessed him, his hard expression, his dark eyes glittering. She had yet to get a good look at his face; from the dim lighting outside, to the even dimmer lighting in here, it made it difficult to assess his features fully. But from what she could tell, he was an exceptionally handsome man. An odd thing to observe about one's captor, but in her line of work observation was everything. He had high cheekbones, a square jaw and a strong chin. The planes and angles of his face cast into sharp relief each time they passed a brightly lit building, or row of streetlights.

"What do you intend for me, then?" It was important to know. Because if he was intending evil things for her she needed to know whether or not she should be trying to fashion a weapon out of the paper clips and Chapstick in the bottom of her purse.

"It's nothing you need to worry about."

"Inconveniently for you, I find I'm exceptionally worried about what exactly a stranger intends to do with me. Even if it is rather mundane. Even if you just intend to ask me about different styles of napkin folding, which I could give you a comprehensive lesson on because I am something of an expert."

"I do not wish to learn to fold napkins."

No, of course he didn't. And she didn't, for one moment, think he had. But it was a better thought than the others swirling in her head. Because as far as she knew, men only had a few things they wanted from women when they removed them from a place forcibly. None of them were any good. None of them were anything she wanted a part of.

She really was in over her head now. She'd wanted to help Isabelle out, and she still did. But she had not realized that digging up scandal on the Chatsfield family to get Spencer Chatsfield off her friend's back would end with her being shoved into a car by an angry stranger. No, indeed, she had imagined she would do a little bit of reconnaissance, and catch James doing what James did. He had been, in her mind, the easiest target.

The Chatsfields were currently making it their mission to take over Harrington Hotels, Spencer Chatsfield doing his best to ruin Isabelle Harrington's life, as if he hadn't already done enough years ago. That was why Isabelle had asked her to do what she could to dig up the scandal on the family, to throw the press a headline bone they couldn't ignore and keep the Chatsfields busy scrambling to cover their butts while Isabelle shored up the defenses for The Harrington.

No, she wasn't exactly a lead reporter for the *Herald*. She was more lead coffee maker and vapid party summarizer for the society pages. But, given that, she had the authority to run a piece on the Chatsfields.

Though, as much as Sophie loved Isabelle, as much as she wanted to help out her friend, she wasn't sure if this was what she signed on for. No, she was certain this wasn't what she'd signed on for.

"So what is it you want?"

"It's quite simple, really. I need to keep you busy for a while."

"I like a scavenger hunt. If you wanted to set up some kind of elaborate game, I might be persuaded to participate. That could keep me busy for a bit."

"That is not what I had in mind."

The hair on the back of her neck stood on end, goose bumps breaking out over her arms. "Organizing your sock drawer?"

"Getting warmer."

"Okay, you need to start talking, because I'm starting to panic."

"Do you know who I am?"

"I have an idea." She had overheard enough of his conversation with James to start piecing some things together. And what she surmised was that he was royalty of some sort. Because he had accused James of sleeping with his sister. His sister, who happened to be a princess. So unless he was some kind of royal bastard, he had to be a prince, sheikh or otherwise titled person. A quick internet search when she'd gotten back to her computer would've clarified everything. Of course, now she was separated from her computer, for who knew how long, so finding out who he was wouldn't be as simple as she imagined.

Though if she could get her phone...

"I am Sheikh Zayn Al-Ahmar, of Surhaadi. And I am taking you back to my country for the foreseeable future."

Her stomach jumped up and hit the back of her throat.

"What do you mean I'm coming back to your country with you?"

"Just exactly what I said. You are returning to Surhaadi with me, until I can figure out a means of dealing with you."

"Well, I don't want to."

He shifted in his seat, one arm draped over the back of it, his legs thrown out in front of him. He had the posture of a lazy cat, as though this were mundane. As though he kidnapped women from alleys in New York every day, and threatened to take them back to his desert kingdom. As though this were as commonplace as ordering sparkling water instead of still.

But she had a feeling it was only an illusion. That, much like a cat, the lazy posture was simply lulling her into a false sense of security, so that she would be all the more surprised when he pounced. She decided then and there that she would not be lulled.

"All of this has very little to do with want, as far as I'm concerned," he said. "Do you truly think I want to bring you back to my country with me? If so, you are mistaken. This goes deeper than want. This is about what I must do."

"Well, what is it you must do? Let me help you with that, and perhaps we can both be spared this whole taking me back to the desert thing."

"I am afraid I do not have time to negotiate."

"I'm asking honestly, what is it you need? What is it you want from me?" Anything was preferable to this. Well, okay, not *anything*. But a lot of things.

"I require your silence, *habibti*. And while under normal circumstances I would be willing to pay for your silence, I find that I must be even more diligent in this instance. I cannot take the chance you will simply take my money and then give away my secrets, anyway."

"I have a lot of honor. And I also have a lot of bills. So, all things considered, a payoff might be your best bet." At this point, she just wanted to forget she had ever even seen the man. No payoff required. She was starting to get seriously freaked out.

"As I said, under normal circumstances I might have gone that route. But there is too much at stake. Anyway, what sort of paltry story do you suppose you could bring out of the Chatsfield name? There is more to this story. More to what I know about James Chatsfield. Come back to the palace with me, and I will tell you everything."

Oh, no, that was far too easy, and made absolutely no sense. The man was trying to get her away from people, away from New York, to keep something secret. He was hardly going to give her surrounding information.

"I don't trust you."

"All things considered, I doubt there is any chance of there being trust between us."

"Well, perhaps we don't need trust. Perhaps we just need you to not force me to go someplace against my will. Right now, I would take that over trust."

The limo started to slow, pulling into a driveway that she didn't recognize. This didn't look like any of the airports she was familiar with, or at least not a terminal she was familiar with. Not that she had spent very much time traveling, but she had dropped friends off when they went on trips.

Still, she was not an authority on air travel. "Where are we?"

"A private section of the airport, reserved for visiting dignitaries. It allows us to sidestep a lot of bureaucracy."

She was starting to put the pieces together, but between the general feeling of shock and the haze of disbelief covering this whole thing she wasn't feeling as quick as she usually did.

"I need you out of the way for a while. Surhaadi is the best place, where I can keep you close. Where I can keep an eye on you. But never fear, you will come away from this rewarded."

A chill spread over her. "I have a job, I have a life, I can't just leave."

Okay, so saying she had a life was pushing it a bit. She had a life of working sixty hours a week, and doing her very best to climb the ladder, such as that was in her industry. She had spent her entire life working her way up from, if not the gutter, certainly a disadvantaged position, to where she was now.

Isabelle Harrington had helped her secure her place at the *Herald*, and Sophie owed her. More than that, she refused to squander any opportunity she was given. The vast majority of the work she had done to elevate her status had been accomplished on her own. Due to nothing more than sheer bloody-mindedness, determination and a burning sense of injustice that sat in her stomach, making her feel hollow. Driving her on, looking for a way to fill it.

But her position at the *Herald* was one of the few things that had been provided for her by her creative friends. Isabelle had recommended her for the position, and Sophie took it very seriously. She didn't take for granted what she had been given. The thought of just leaving the job, for an indefinite amount of time, was unthinkable.

"Where is it you work?"

"I work at the *New York Herald*, and I can't just leave."

"I will call your boss, and I will speak to him."

"Uh…no. You won't. That is not happening." Knowing Colin, he would smell a story and be no help in bailing her out. Her boss had the morals of a vulture. He was opportunistic in the extreme. A man who had attached himself to a very wealthy wife, using those connections to land himself a position as head editor for the *Herald*, all while sleeping with younger social-ites behind her back.

He was opportunistic, but not, in Sophie's experience, particularly sneaky. Either way, she did not want to bring him into this.

"You have now told me where you work. I am more than happy to take the ID out of your bag, find your name and call your boss. I will tell him that one of his reporters has greatly offended the sheikh of Surhaadi. And I will tell him I want you fired."

Fear streaked through her. She despised it. Despised this feeling of being so disadvantaged because she was, by birth, *lesser*.

But I shouldn't be. I should be one of them. But because my father didn't choose me...

"You don't actually think that would work, do you?"

"I do not see why it wouldn't."

"Well, perhaps in any other industry, it would work. But this is the media, if you give any hint of a scandal, they'll just want to know what the scandal is. No one is going to fire me for creating a little bit of dust between myself and a sheikh."

"You see, that is where you're wrong. Because I have the capability of offering them a much bigger story than you ever could with your half-heard findings in the alleyway. But I would make it contingent upon them letting you go. And rest assured they would."

"I can't believe this. Are you seriously going to get me fired from my job? Because of…just because I overheard that Chatsfield slept with your sister?"

"Yes," he said, his voice grave. "I would do just that. Do not doubt it. There are two things in this life that are dear to me. My people, and my family. I will do whatever is necessary to protect them. Sometimes, when you are the ruler of the country, that means being willing to go to war. When you are the head of the family, that means being willing to wage war on a more personal scale." His gaze met hers, and even in the darkness of the car, she could feel the righteous fury emanating from him, could feel the heat. "There is nothing I would not do to protect my family. And right now, I feel that my hand is being forced."

"I'm not forcing anything."

"Your very presence does. Your name?"

"Why should I tell you?" He gave her a hard look, one that told her he would get it one way or another. She would just tell him. At least then it would be her choice. "Sophie Parsons."

"And who do you report to directly?"

"Colin Fairfax."

"Phone number?"

She rattled it off, because at this point, if she had her boss on the other end of the phone, perhaps she could at least signal her distress. Sheikh whatever-his-name-was retrieved the phone from the interior pocket of his jacket, and dialed the number she had given. A moment later she heard the phone stop ringing on the other end, and heard her boss's voice coming through the line, muffled but recognizable.

"Yes, I am calling about an employee of yours. Sophie Parsons."

She could hear words, but not what they were.

"She has done nothing wrong. She is with me, in fact…Sheikh Zayn, of Surhaadi…Yes, that one. We got into a bit of a discussion, and we spoke about her coming to Surhaadi to run a piece on my upcoming marriage."

The implications of what he was saying turned over in her mind, and for the first time, she realized that some of this could actually go her way. That she could get something out of this.

Except where Isabelle is concerned. You're leaving Isabelle up a creek without a paddle.

Not that she was doing it on purpose. If she had her way, she would escape the limo and run screaming into the night. But she didn't seem to have much choice. He would load her onto the plane kicking and screaming if he had to, of *that* she had no doubt. There was barely another living soul out here, at least no one who didn't work for him. And he had her boss on the line, her job in his hands, and if she did not have access to the media, the help that she could be to Isabelle was limited, anyway.

No, she wasn't deserting her friend for self-serving reasons. She wasn't deserting her friend for any reason that was in her control.

"She is a very charming young woman," Zayn continued. "I find myself captivated by her. I should like to read her perspective of the goings-on."

Her boss responded, his voice sounding much more cheerful and genial than it ever did when he spoke to her. Probably because she was a gopher and not a sheikh.

"I am not certain how long I will have her in Surhaadi, but of course we do have internet connections, and she will be able to make contact." Somehow, Sophie doubted he would allow her free contact.

"Yes, I daresay it will be a wonderful exclusive for your paper. She will be in touch soon." Zayn hung up, putting the phone back inside his jacket pocket. "There, that was relatively painless, wasn't it?"

"For you, perhaps. I find all this has been quite painful."

"I have scarcely laid a finger on you."

"Pain can come in a lot of forms. Often I find the physical is the least of my worries." That much was true, she had enough emotional garbage to last a lifetime.

"Well, it is all settled, your boss is happy to have you come to Surhaadi with me. And if you refuse, I will not hesitate to call him back and let him know you blew the story, and that I will require your immediate termination if the paper is to get the exclusive that I have now promised."

"So those are my options? Be carried onto the plane kicking and screaming and lose my job, or get on the plane and keep my job."

"That about sums it up."

"What about my scandal? I need to do this. If you think I was out here for my own gratification, you're wrong. I'm doing this for someone else. For a friend, and it's important."

"Come with me, and you will have your scandal." His dark eyes were fathomless, impossible to read. But she could also see that she had no choice but to go with him.

She swallowed hard, trying to combat the swarm of nerves crawling through her system like a hoard of ants. "Then I guess we are going to Surhaadi."

* * *

Zayn's private plane was far more luxurious than anything Sophie had been exposed to before. And in the years since she'd moved up from her nondescript existence in a quiet neighborhood, tucked away from people she and her mother might encounter who would know who her father was, she had seen a fair bit of luxury.

She had not, however, seen private plane levels of luxury.

She felt like it had to be some kind of mental disconnect happening within her brain right now. Because she was essentially being kidnapped, and yet she was admiring the butter-soft quality of the leather that covered the chairs that were stationed throughout the airplane cabin.

All things considered, she didn't feel like this was the time to be admiring the qualities of leather. Though if she thought about anything much deeper she might go insane. Because all of this was just too much to digest at once. She needed time to get used to this whole being kidnapped by a sheikh thing.

"There are two bedrooms in the back of the plane, and you're welcome to use whichever one you like," he said, speaking as though he was playing host at an extremely civilized dinner party. "You are also welcome to stay up here should you prefer. Can I get you a drink?"

"Well, the offer of the bedroom is certainly appreciated. As is the offer of a drink. Which I accept."

She had never been much for drinking. After Isabelle had accepted her into her group of friends, Sophie had often found herself dining in places that were way above her pay grade. Soup or salad, coupled with the water, had often been the only thing on her menu. Certainly, had her friend been aware of the fact that Sophie couldn't afford the places they'd gone, Isabelle would have happily given Sophie the money to pay for her meal. But charity had never sat well with Sophie. And anyway, the burning hunger to one day be able to order the fish dish, rather than ordering from the appetizer section, was one of the things that kept her going.

She had often been afraid that if she took those kinds of incentives from herself she would lose some of her drive. And that, in her mind, was unacceptable.

Of course, a fish-based entrée was not the be-all and end-all to her ambition. She'd worked for what she had. Every single bit of prestige and education. She'd gained tentative acceptance, acceptance that would have simply been her due had she been one of her father's legitimate children.

The university she had attended had been a given for her half siblings. Something they could simply have because of their parentage. While she had not been afforded the same.

Because she and her mother had been secret. Because she and her mother had been kept separate. So she had set out to prove that she didn't need her father's influence, or money. She had worked her way to university on her own, graduating in the top of her class with a degree in journalism.

Three years on, and now that she was doing very little else beyond making coffee for the *Herald*, some of that triumph had dwindled.

But she was determined to hold on to her ambition. Because it had gotten her this far. Because it was the only thing she had to get her the rest of the way.

Which was why she couldn't curl into a ball and give up now. This was the only way she could figure out how to help Isabelle, anyway. The sheikh claimed to know more than he let on, and she had to find out what it was he knew. She was stuck with him for a while, then.

And her boss now expected a profile of the royal wedding in Surhaadi. Which meant she might as well take in the whole experience. A certain amount of observation, including the quality of the leather, would be required of her.

She was, after all, a journalist. And so, she was hardly working to her full capacity at the moment as to what she intended to be one day. What was it they said? Dress for the job you want, not the job you have.

Well, right now, she would be taking in details, acting the part of the journalist she wanted to be, rather than the journalist she was. True, all of this had a bit more of a society bent than she cared for. She was interested in, someday, taking on stories that might be a little more hard-hitting than a sheikh's upcoming marriage. But this was several rungs up the ladder she was currently standing on, and she would be foolish if she didn't just go ahead and embrace it.

Frankly, she was kidnapped either way.

"What do you prefer?" he asked.

"Oh, something red, I should think. Do you drink white for a kidnapping?"

"I would think most people would prefer something a little bit stiffer for their kidnapping."

"So, you admit that you're kidnapping me."

He wandered over to an ornate covered bar that was set into the wall, bottles closed into shelves, secured into carved wooden holders. He opened the doors, and selected a bottle of wine. "I do not see the point in quibbling over semantics. It changes nothing either way."

"Well, one allows me a little bit of justified anger."

"I do not see what you have to be angry about. Unless you have a lover you are meant to meet tonight."

The very idea was ridiculous. She didn't do the whole man-woman thing. Who had the time? Or the inclination toward heartbreak. Maybe, when she got to where she was going, maybe, if she ever found a man she thought she might be able to trust. Maybe. Two very big maybes.

"My diary for the evening was free," she said.

"Then I would imagine that, as a journalist, a drink on a private plane with royalty makes for a much better story than you sitting on your couch and watching sitcoms."

He had a point. But she wasn't going to tell him that.

"I'm sure, but in the end most of this will make for a very good story. So what exactly am I supposed to be covering? You mentioned there being more to the Chatsfield scandal, but since then you've been awfully quiet about it."

She could hear the engines of the plane being fired up, and her stomach flipped. She wasn't used to flying. She had done a little bit domestically, but certainly nothing international. She didn't even know how to calculate the estimated length of the flight from New York to Surhaadi.

"James Chatsfield is an ass. You can quote me directly on that, if you would like."

"Forgive me, Sheikh Zayn, but there is full documentation proving that about James Chatsfield already. It's hardly breaking news."

The plane started to move down the runway and she wobbled where she stood. "You may want to sit down."

And with that, it was clear the subject was closed. She did not find that acceptable in the least.

"Don't *you* want to sit down?" she asked.

"I have a drink to pour."

She walked across the expanse of the plane, and took a seat in one of the chairs. They were, indeed, as soft as they looked. Just for her mental records. For when she was writing a piece on this experience. On what it had been like to be in the private plane of the sheikh of Surhaadi.

He poured her a very full glass of red, not even looking unsteady when the plane picked up momentum. Then he put a stopper back in the bottle, and put it back in the cabinet. Before walking nonchalantly across the cabin and handing her the glass. He took a seat across from her, his hands noticeably empty of a drink.

"I think you and I have a lot in common, re-

ally. We both want Chatsfield blood. I think you
should help me get some." She took a sip of the
wine, and fought to keep her expression neutral.
This was not cheap wine.

If she ever did buy herself wine for home, it
usually came in mini-bottles or a box. Silk taste,
polyester budget and all that.

"Later. Later you will have your scandal. For
now we can talk wedding business."

Irritation spiked through her, and she fought
to keep from showing him, fought to keep from
revealing her hand any more than she already
had. "But you *are* getting married? That's true,
right?"

"Yes, I am."

She noticed he didn't sound overjoyed at the
mention of the upcoming union. She would file
that away, as well. She would also continue
down this line of questioning, because he was
being a bit more forthcoming on this topic than
on the topic of the Chatsfields.

She shifted in her seat, crossing her legs, and
holding the wine out over the cream-colored
carpet as the plane started to ascend. She didn't
have very many nice dresses, and she would
be darned if she was going to get a red wine
stain on one of the few she did own. His carpet
would pay the price before this sequined mas-
terpiece did.

"When is the wedding?"

A strange-looking smile curved the corners of his lips. It was not a happy expression, neither did it hold very much humor. "Three weeks."

That would likely put her right at the center of the action. In spite of herself, she did find that exciting. "I imagine a lot of the preparation is under way already."

"While my staff is executing much of it, my fiancée is dictating the activity from her home country."

"She isn't from Surhaadi?"

"No. My fiancée is the princess of a small European country. The fourth-born child in the family, and the only girl. She is still living in the palace there."

"Long-distance relationship, understandable. Though not ideal."

He shrugged. "I find nothing terribly un-ideal about it. There is no reason for Christine to uproot her life prior to our union becoming official."

"Some people might not consider it very inconvenient to uproot things for the person they love."

"Who said anything about love?" His dark eyes connected with hers and sent a shock wave down to her stomach. She took a deep breath, trying to ignore it.

She supposed she of all people shouldn't have inferred love into a conversation about marriage. She hardly thought her own father loved the woman he was married to. Now, she didn't suppose that the man loved her mother, either, but he certainly didn't love his wife. If he did, why would he conduct so many affairs? Why would he conduct affairs with anyone at all?

"I don't suppose anyone did. Except for me."

"It is not a secret that my union with Christine has more to do with politics than feelings."

"Oh, but the world loves a love match." She leaned back in her seat, lifting her wineglass to her lips. "I should very much doubt if the public is content to imagine that you are simply allies for politics and not for pleasure."

A political union would not make for a very strong hook in her piece. A piece she would have to give some consideration to, regardless of her primary aim of interviewing Zayn. Because Colin was expecting a story about a royal wedding now, and she had to deliver.

That wasn't a problem, though, she was used to multitasking. Unlike most of her peers she'd had to hold on to a part-time job while going to school. And again, unlike most of her classmates, there had been no job waiting for her when she graduated. So there had been internships, combined with late shifts waitressing at bars.

No, multitasking wasn't a problem for her.

"Yes, I daresay the public will be disappointed on that score."

"Unless you decide to show them something else."

"To what end?" He looked at her, and she could see that he was clearly intrigued.

"To the end of positive public opinion. Which I should think for a world leader would be of the utmost importance." She knew all about playing that game, because in her life presenting a positive front, presenting a polished front, had been imperative.

Most everyone she'd gone to university with were simply accepted, based on their names and connections, but she hadn't had that. Sophie had been forced to earn respect. She hadn't been able to afford the mistakes the rest of her friends had been allowed to make. Any slip-up in behavior for them could be perceived as a simple youthful rebellion. For her, it was a revealing window into just how unsophisticated she was. Just how unsuitable she was. It was proof that, as they all expected, she didn't belong.

For those reasons she'd had to be above reproach, because she was starting at a place of disadvantage.

Yes, Sophie knew all about manipulating public opinion—or in her case, the opinion of university administration and her fellow students—to her advantage.

"It certainly is, but shouldn't my efforts to improve relations between countries count for something?"

"Certainly, and I'm sure for some it will. But it will be lost on others. And while they might accept your union with a kind of blissful neutrality, or at least a bit of interest in what your bride will be wearing, they would be a lot more interested in romance."

"Then I give you leave to infer romance to your heart's content when you write your piece."

Sophie took another sip of wine. "I promise to read between the lines judiciously."

"By which you mean you promise to read things that aren't there?"

"That is a particular specialty of those who report on high-society stories."

For the first time since he'd pulled her unceremoniously from the alley, the corners of his lips turned upward into a smile. It was not a smile that expressed happiness, but rather one that seemed to be laughing at some kind of perverse amusement. He rubbed his hand across his chin, fingertips grazing his square jaw, and she found herself distracted by the sound of his skin rubbing against the dark stubble. It was a very masculine thing, and she had not been exposed to many masculine things in her life.

An all-female household, female roommates, until she finally got her tiny apartment and lived alone.

Men were something of a foreign animal to her, and as she looked across to the man sitting opposite her, she realized he was an extremely foreign animal indeed.

He was magnetic, his features strong, dark brows, a blade-straight nose, eyes the color of midnight, framed by sooty lashes, the sort of lips that would entice lesser women to compose poetry about them.

Had he any softness to him, he might've been called beautiful. But he did not, so she would not. *Beautiful* wasn't the right word.

Powerful, that was the word. The kind of power that far exceeded most of the people she'd been exposed to. No matter how influential a society family in New York might be, a sheikh certainly outstripped them.

He was the sort of man with ultimate power, not a man ruled by the laws of this, or any, land, really. Beneath his well-tailored suit, she could sense he was a man who didn't ascribe to civility in a typical sense. Well, her presence on this plane was proof enough of that.

He was dangerous, she realized with a sudden jolt. And for some reason, she found that more fascinating than repulsing. She couldn't figure out why.

She would attribute that to the masculine inexperience thing. Because it was easier than having to examine it deeper. This way, she could stick it in the "men are mystery" drawer and close it tight.

She suddenly became very aware of the fact that her heart was beating faster than normal. She would ignore that, too.

"Yes, I am well aware that it is a skill of the press, to imply all kinds of things." The smile stayed fixed on his face, but there was a darkness to it now. A terrifying emptiness that was reflected in his eyes.

"In this case, perhaps it will benefit you."

The smile widened, and she felt an answering tightness in her chest, as though he had managed to forge a link between his facial expressions and her insides. As though he had not just kidnapped her body, but had seized control over other parts of her. It was disconcerting, to say the least.

"Perhaps it will benefit both of us in the end."

CHAPTER THREE

NOTHING COULD HAVE prepared her for the over-
whelming heat of Surhaadi. The arid wind that
had whipped across her face as she made her
way down the staircase from the plane into the
waiting limo had been dry and hot like an oven.
Her pale skin starting to burn the moment she
got beneath the sun's rays.

In truth, it felt as though they were closer to
the sun here than they had been in New York.
It was beyond anything in her experience, and
while it was uncomfortable, it was also fascinating.

Her level of fascination with her new surroundings far surpassed the unease she had been
feeling on the plane ride over. She'd managed to
sleep for a good portion of the flight, disengaging herself from conversation with Zayn after
their little talk about love matches. For some
reason, being close to him made her feel jittery.

Okay, so it was normal to feel jittery around

the man who'd essentially forced her to come back to his country with him, but this was something else. Something that went beyond the expected unease that one might feel in the situation.

And she was still ignoring it. Ignoring it, and focusing on the view of the Surhaadi desert, and then, of the looming palace walls, and the massive structure that rose up from behind them.

Every window in the palace seemed to be lit with an orange flame, each line, every detail of stone carved into the walls, illuminated by a thin band of light. A blue dome rose from the center of the roof, an intricate pattern fashioned from the gleaming tile that covered it.

It was a modern-day fantasy. An updated take on classic stories that she'd read as a child.

But sadly reading about it could not have prepared her for the reality. For the sheer size of the place.

Yet again, going to friends' holiday homes upstate was a poor comparison to the home of actual royalty.

"What do you think?" he asked as the limo drove through the parting gates and into a beautifully appointed courtyard, the ground covered in gleaming tile, and fountains stationed throughout.

"I suppose it will have to do," she said, her tone dry as the desert sand.

"I daresay not many people get kidnapped into such luxury."

"That all depends, I suppose, on whether or not you intend to throw me in the dungeon."

"You shall have your own quarters."

Her own quarters in a massive palace. Things continued to seem unreal. "Oh."

"No matter what you might think, I am not an animal. I am simply a man. Doing what I must to ensure that my family remains safe."

She wasn't familiar with that kind of loyalty. And for a moment, the desire to be on the receiving end of it, from someone, anyone, *him* even, was so strong it made her ache.

What would it be like to have someone do whatever must be done, to protect you?

She and her mother had never been close, and they had only grown more distant throughout the years. Her mother had no ambition beyond being a rich man's plaything. Worse, as the years had gone on, she hadn't even been the rich man's plaything, but his discarded toy. And she had never moved on from that. She'd never been able to connect with her only child, because her heart had been given over to a man who didn't care about her at all.

Sophie would have loved her. But she'd never given Sophie the chance.

And Sophie hadn't been able to watch her mother endure that existence after a certain point, either.

And as for her father, she may as well have not existed. Except for a card, with a check, on every birthday. A check she had summarily put into savings and hadn't touched until her university years.

This kind of familial love, this kind of protectiveness, wasn't something she had any experience with.

It was best to just focus on the palace.

"So, is this the original palace? Or is this something of a redo?"

"There have been extensive renovations in the past twenty years. Lots of modernizing. But the majority of it is original. A couple hundred years old. Of course, while homes that are that age are magnificent, they are rarely comfortable to live in. Hence the renovation."

"Sure, I imagine that's the case."

She knew for a fact that living in a home that was fifty years old wasn't overly comfortable, so anything spanning back centuries probably wasn't any better. Though it looked immeasurably fancier.

The limousine came to a stop, and Zayn got

out without waiting for a driver to come to his aid. He walked to her side of the car, and opened the door for her, standing there as though he was some kind of chivalrous paragon, rather than the marauder she knew he was.

She collected her purse, and got out, rising slowly, her body a little bit stiff from such a long plane ride followed by a ride in a car. The wind whipped through her hair, and she flicked some of the honey strands away from her face, the sun reflecting on it and casting a golden haze over her vision.

He stood tall, regarding her, his expression like granite.

"What?" she asked.

"Just thinking about how strange it is."

"What?"

"How quickly things can change."

She lifted her shoulder. "I feel like that should be something I'm pondering more than you."

"I know you feel quite inconvenienced by all of this. But you must realize that it is a difficulty for me, as well."

"No, I really don't think I have to acknowledge that."

"I wasn't prepared to host a guest. And I have a wedding to plan."

"Forgive me for feeling short on apologies at

the moment. I find I'm not all that sympathetic to your fate."

Yet again, she earned one of his odd smiles. "No, I imagine you wouldn't be. Follow me, I will escort you to your room."

He turned away from her, and started to walk toward the palace without waiting for her. She took a deep breath, and scampered after him, having to take two steps to his every one to try and keep up, last night's high heels feeling like bricks nailed to the soles of her feet after so many hours in them.

She estimated that he was nearly a foot taller than her own five foot four, her head landing just below his shoulder. And he was broad, incredibly muscular with a trim waist and...

Again, just filing away details about him, for when she wrote her piece on the wedding. It had nothing to do with her own personal need to catalog details about him.

The double doors to the palace swung open, as if by magic, and the two were admitted into the cool antechamber.

Dimly, she realized that comparing the doors to magic was a bit silly. Had they been in a shopping mall, automatic doors would not have seemed at all out of place. It was this place, this strange mix of old and new, of fairy tale and blazing-hot reality, that had her creating fanciful metaphors in her head.

Inside, there were members of what she assumed to be palace staff milling around, but if the presence of their ruler was notable, they didn't show any sign of it. They moved around like they were ghosts, intent on being invisible to anyone in the land of the living. And Zayn did not appear to notice them at all. So that, she assumed, was palace protocol.

The help going unnoticed, the antics of their ruler going unnoticed, too, apparently. Because nobody seemed to blink over the fact that their sheikh had just walked into the palace with an unknown woman trailing behind him. An unknown woman wearing a sequined party dress quite early in the day. Truly, no one seemed concerned at all.

"I made a phone call from the plane while you were sleeping, and had your room prepared for you."

So, they *were* expecting her. Or at least whoever had made her bed was expecting her. Though she imagined they made it a practice not to question their orders too deeply.

"Well, I will happily allow you to lead me there." She felt suddenly stale from travel. As though her body had been folded and packed away tightly in a suitcase for the duration of the journey.

She needed to get out of the dress and into something a little bit less constricting.

And that was when it occurred to her that she didn't have any clothes. Nothing at all. She didn't even have a toothbrush.

"I don't have anything to wear."

He didn't answer. He didn't even pause.

Zayn was pressing through the antechamber, barely looking at anything or anyone, or at the opulent surroundings. Though she imagined this was all commonplace to him.

But nothing about this was commonplace to her, from the ornate mosaics on the floor and walls, to the marble pillars placed throughout the room to the ceilings inlaid with precious stones.

The palace was like a jewelry box, more than a dwelling. Evidence of riches beyond her wildest dreams built into the framework.

She imagined if she took a chisel and mallet to one of the walls she would come away from them with enough gold dust to pay her rent for the next couple of months.

He led her down a narrow passageway that fed into another massive room with two curving staircases on either side. He paused for a moment, then turned to face her. "This way."

He started up the staircase on the left side of the room, his footsteps almost silent on the stone. She did her best to keep up with him, her heels echoing loudly in the empty, cavernous room. She was not quite as stealthy as he was.

"This is the part of the palace that is often reserved for visiting dignitaries. And members of the press."

"From my limited research on Surhaadi," she said, speaking to his back, "I didn't think you had a lot of visitors. Dignitaries, press or otherwise."

"Not in recent years, no."

"If by recent years you mean the past decade and a half."

"For a family as old as mine, that is recent years. In the fabric of history, fifteen years is nothing."

She cleared her throat. "Well, in the fabric of my lifetime, fifteen years is quite a bit."

He paused, the expression on his face strange. "How old are you?"

"Twenty-five."

He stopped walking and swore, the sound harsh. "Barely older than my sister."

"Is that a problem?" She could tell from the look on his face that it was.

"It is very young."

"I wouldn't lose any sleep over it. I imagine

in many ways I'm years older than your sister, and in fact many years older than you might assume someone my age would be."

"What's that supposed to mean?"

"Exactly what it sounds like. People in your position have the luxury of clinging to their innocence a lot longer than people in mine."

He laughed, the sound hollow, reverberating off the walls. "I have never been accused of being innocent."

He turned away from her again, and continued walking down the corridor, and she took a deep breath, and went after him, doing her best to keep up. "Would you care to elaborate?"

"Do I hear a hint of the journalist in your tone?"

"You ought to. It's the only reason I'm here."

"That, and you were essentially forced into coming."

"For the sake of my pride, let's not speak of that." Not that one really had any pride to speak of when one was tromping down the hall after a stranger in last night's dress, trying not to twist an ankle on the uneven mosaic floor.

"Well, then, for your pride."

"My pride thanks you," she said, her tone dry.

"Somehow I doubt it."

"I'm trying to make small talk," she said.

"Perhaps it's best if you don't."

It seemed that this area of the palace was deserted. Such a strange thing. Especially when she knew there had to be hundreds of members of staff and residents. Especially when the house she'd grown up in could easily fit inside one of the large antechambers.

The cavernous, empty feel was kind of unsettling.

They came to the end of the hallway and he stopped at a pair of double doors, inlaid with gold and jade. They were a stunning piece of art, rather than just a means of entry or exit.

"This is your room."

He didn't make a move to open the door, so she cautiously reached past him and pushed it open.

Calling it a mere room was a grave disservice. It was a suite of rooms, with a plush seating area in front, and great pillars dividing it into sections, separating it from a raised bedroom area at the back. The bed was large and plush, swaths of fabric hanging from the ceiling, sweeping outward before being caught by an ornate golden canopy that guided the lush silk to the floor.

To the right, through a domed entryway, she could see what looked like a bathing chamber. Not a mere bathroom, that was way too tame of a description for a room so grand, with what looked like a sunken bathtub that was larger than some backyard pools.

Zayn turned to face her. "I trust you will find everything you need here. And if not, do not hesitate to ask a member of staff, or myself, for something that might make you more comfortable."

"A computer with internet?"

He shook his head. "Anything but that."

"Satellite phone?"

"You can't have that, either."

She tapped her chin. "So when you said anything…"

"I meant a cold drink, or shoes in a different size or color."

"Wait… Shoes?"

He looked down at her feet, at the platform high heels that were starting to make her feel achy all the way up her calves. "I thought that you might be in need of something else to wear."

"Well, you're not wrong. But did you seriously…buy clothes for me?"

"I had my sister's personal shopper do it, but yes."

"And how do you know what size I wear?"

"I took a guess. And anything that doesn't fit can be returned."

"You did not take a guess at what size my feet were."

He shrugged. "All right, I looked at the bottom of your shoe when you were sleeping on the couch in the plane. I could see the number. But your dress size I did take a guess on."

The thought of just what him guessing her dress size might entail sent a shiver through her. He would have had to look at her awfully closely. Taken visual measurements...

She closed off that line of thinking, and quickly. "Well, indeed."

He inclined his head. "I will leave you now, you are formally invited to dinner tonight."

"And at dinner we discuss the scandal?"

"All in good time." Then he turned and walked from the room, leaving her standing there alone.

She took a breath. No offer of shoes, or pretty clothes, could be allowed to distract her from what she was doing here, she had to remember that. The wedding was window dressing, the beauty of the palace was window dressing, *everything* but the Chatsfield scandal was window dressing.

Isabelle had done so much for her. Without her, Sophie doubted she would've ever found her place at university. She doubted if she would have ever made friends at all. She certainly wouldn't have her job at the *Herald*. More than that, Isabelle had been a true friend to her, regardless of where Sophie had come from. And that was something Sophie couldn't put a price on.

She owed her this now. Isabelle had been through enough at the hands of Spencer Chatsfield, and the idea of her losing The Harrington was inconceivable.

She would not allow it. If she could play even a small part in preventing it from happening, she would.

And she would not be distracted.

Now, she just had to get cleaned up, and begin to feel human again. Then she could choose something to wear for dinner. She really hoped that there was something stunning in the closet. Because she had a feeling she would need it to feel confident. She had a feeling that interviewing Zayn would be a lot like going into battle.

And that meant she needed to get her armor on.

She went to the closet and examined the contents. Inside she saw a rainbow of fine fabrics, the lush textures denoting a quality that she could scarcely believe was at her fingertips. A quality that she was, frankly, almost afraid to put her fingertips on.

The kinds of clothes she passed in a store with barely a glance because she knew she couldn't afford them, and she always had a feeling the store employees knew it, too.

She reached out and laid a hand on a dress that was a vibrant orange and an involuntary breath escaped her lips.

This was the one.

As she took her clothes off and got ready to slip the dress on, she had a sudden fear that it wouldn't fit. But she pulled it up over her hips and contorted, sliding the zipper up, and found that it conformed perfectly to her curves.

He had indeed guessed accurately. Again, she got all weird and tingly thinking about what the guessing entailed. She shook her head and turned, coming face-to-face with her reflection in the vanity mirror.

And she lost her breath.

Standing here in a castle, in a dress that fit like a dream. Like magic mice and birds had tailored it to suit her, or a fairy godmother had conjured it up using nothing but silk and magic.

She turned away sharply, her heart hammering hard. She was being an idiot. This wasn't a fairy tale. She wasn't the maid-turned-princess. She was a journalist. She was a friend. And she did not have time to indulge in fantasy.

She had a job to do.

CHAPTER FOUR

ZAYN WAS UNPREPARED for the sight that greeted him when he entered the dining room that night. Sophie was already there, seated next to the head of the table.

She was a far cry from the woman he had found crouched behind trash cans in the alley. Certainly, it had been apparent she was beautiful even then, but just now she was somewhere beyond beautiful.

Radiant was one word that could be used to describe her. If he was given to such flights of fancy, and he was not.

Her golden hair was piled on top of her head, giving the impression of a halo, which was laughable all things considered.

Her face was made up, but done so in a very subtle way. Her cheeks glowed, an iridescent shimmer around her eyes brightening the green of them. Her lips were slick with some kind of pale pink gloss.

But it was the dress that she wore that made

him want to call his sister's personal shopper and fire her on the spot. Not because it wasn't perfect, but because it was too perfect.

The burnished orange fabric molded itself to her skin, the structured bodice cupping her breasts, drawing his eyes to them. It was the dress, and not him, and certainly not her. Because he had been celibate for nearly three years now, ever since his engagement had been made official. And in all that time, he had never had any trouble keeping his eyes where they ought to be. He respected women, he did not see them as tools for his personal pleasure, or visual enjoyment. He did not leer at them when he invited them to join him for dinner.

That meant the only answer was that the dress was sincerely inappropriate. Because *he* was most certainly not. He had been nothing but appropriate for a great many years now. And he was hardly going to start changing his ways now.

"I did not expect you to be here already." He strode past her, and took his seat at the head of the table.

"I thought I would spend some time taking in the sights. Getting oriented. I made it to the dining room a little quicker than anticipated."

"I hope you haven't been waiting long."

"No, I haven't."

"I trust a member of staff has already been by to collect your drink order?"

She smiled, her lush lips curving upward. "I have been expertly cared for, thank you."

"Good," he said, his eyes fixed on her.

Last night there had been no time to notice just how beautiful she was, because he had been too busy trying to figure out what he was going to do with her.

Now suddenly he had noticed, and his body had a whole different idea as to what one might do with her.

No question, his captive was lovely. It was a shame he didn't trust her. It was a shame that her loveliness simply couldn't come into play. He was not in that place in his life. And even if he was, she would be the last person on earth he would ever touch.

She was privy to pieces of information that, were they ever connected, would bring press attention he did not need. Or want.

"I suppose I shouldn't have expected you to serve my drink when we were here in the palace. But I got used to my royal treatment on the plane." She sounded sincere enough, but he wasn't fooled. She was angry with him. And he knew she had every right to be. But it did not mean he felt any remorse over his actions.

He'd had to act, there was no question about

that. And her staying in the Surhaadi palace for a while would hardly damage her.

There was the slight issue of the fact that he would not be giving her any additional information on the Chatsfields, if for no other reason than he didn't have any. But she didn't need to know that. He simply needed to keep her here until the wedding.

By then, Leila would've made a decision, by then the media would be distracted with the proceedings. Yes, he needed to keep her here for three weeks, and then things would take care of themselves. She would return to New York with the story that her boss wanted, and his family would be safe.

He could not subject them to the kind of firestorm that had happened when Jasmine, his other sister, had died. That had been his fault, a failure on his part to protect her, and this with Leila was no different. He would handle it better.

Because he was not the same stupid boy he had been. He did not only care for himself and his pleasure; to the contrary, his pleasure took a backseat to everything else. He had a duty to fulfill, both to his country, and his family. He would never fail in that, never again.

He would be damned if he allowed a media firestorm to force Leila's hand. That meant as far as Sophie was concerned, he had to keep his wits about him. There was no time for him to allow her dress to distract him.

It was everything. It was the essence of who he was.

"I think I will allow the staff to serve us both tonight."

As if on cue a member of staff appeared not only with her drink, but with his. She had ordered wine, and they had brought one for him, as well. He was not a devout man, his faith left crumbled and scattered somewhere in his debauched past, and he did often drink a glass of wine with dinner. However, given the fact that his control seemed to be closer to the edge than usual, he was wondering if it was a wise decision.

He accepted the glass, a feeling of determination blooming in his chest and spreading outward. He would not allow her to control the situation. Not in regards to what he drank, or ate, or did. He was not a slave to his body, or her dress.

He leaned back in the chair, keeping his eyes on her, on the way her fingertips slid uneasily along the stem of her wineglass. It was a small display of nerves, but he would take it. Would take it as a sign that he was very much in control.

"I do hope you don't have any particular dietary restrictions." He regarded her closely.

"Such as?"

"Vegetarian, gluten-free."

"I don't. But thank you for asking."

"Well, don't thank me prematurely. I was about to tell you that if you do I will not be able to accommodate you tonight, but tomorrow and the evenings thereafter we would have."

"Thankfully, there is nothing to accommodate. So, I thank you again, for your thoughtfulness."

"Have you poisoned my wine?"

"Why would you ask such a thing?" Her green eyes were wide, the essence of wounded innocence. He didn't buy it for a moment.

"You are being awfully nice considering your current situation. Much nicer than you were only hours ago."

"I'm being professional. This is a professional meal, isn't it?"

He lifted his wineglass to his lips. "I see."

"Do you? What is it you see, exactly?"

"I see that you are ready to play the game."

"This is the game, this is my career. And beyond that, this is a friend's livelihood at stake."

"Interesting. What does your friend's livelihood have to do with any of this?" She looked away from him, biting her lip. "I see, you have given away more than you intended to. This is very interesting."

"The only thing you need to know is that we have a common enemy," she said, looking up, her eyes blazing now. "I don't think either of us are James Chatsfield's biggest fan. As far as I can see, that's all either of us need to know. For now."

"For now."

The double doors to the dining room opened again, and more staff entered, with platters laden with food. They set them down in the center of the table, they did not speak, as the palace staff here in Surhaadi were trained to do. In his own quarters, he treated staff differently. When he had lived predominantly in the other palace, things had been structured differently. But this was the way his father had run things, and the way his mother preferred to run things, as well. And while they were no longer in residence here, the established protocol remained the same.

They were served in silence, and both he and Sophie let the silence rest. Once their plates were filled, and the staff had filed back out again, she turned her sharp green eyes to him. "You promised me an interview. You promised me a scandal. I would like to collect on that now."

"During dinner? I do not conduct business during dinner." That was a lie, he had conducted business during dinner plenty of times, but he did not like her dictating the terms. And he also needed to figure out how to keep her interested for the next few weeks. There was also the small matter of what he was going to tell her.

The simple fact was, he had no information on James Chatsfield he was willing to share. That was the sort of scandal she was after, and it was not one he could give. Which meant he was going to have to lead her on a journey that would not end where she expected..

He just hadn't decided where yet.

"It is a very good dinner. But I did anticipate getting down to things. We traveled quite a lot, and I am feeling tired."

"Do you want your story? Or not?"

"Obviously I do."

"Then you will wait and you will hear it on my terms."

He could read the annoyance plainly on her face, and he found it perversely enjoyable. Yet another point in his win column. Yet more evidence that he was still in command, no matter how well fitted her dress was.

"Tell me, then," she said, looking back up at him, attempting to look friendly, but still looking like she would rather sink her teeth into his neck. Unfortunately, something about that image sent a sharp jolt of heat straight to his gut. He ignored it.

She cleared her throat. "Which topics are on the table for dinner? So that I know for future evenings."

"We may discuss the weather, though, invariably it is hot."

"The weather is hot, there we have covered that."

"Very well done." He took a bite of couscous, and let the conversation rest until he was finished. "We may also discuss issues of the day. I see no reason why we ought not to occasionally discuss politics, or even religion. Seeing as I doubt either of us are worried about offending each other."

"True, after you take control of someone's person and force them to come back to their country with you, you have sort of made it clear that you don't care whether or not you offend them. But I do wonder if discussing politics might get dicey, as the fact remains that if we discuss politics in Surhaadi, we will be discussing you."

"Then we can stick to American politics."

She laughed, a short, one-note sound. "No, that's something I can't discuss while eating, for fear I will be sick," she said, her tone dry.

"Fair enough. Perhaps I will take this oppor-

tunity to ask you about you." He didn't really
care about his beautiful captive, neither should
he. She was a liability, and she needed to be
minimized. That was what one did when something was a liability. It did not matter where
she came from, or who her friend was that she
seemed to be intent on protecting. It did not
matter if she had a lover, or if she did not.

All that mattered was protecting Leila.

"And what is it exactly you want to know
about me?" she asked.

"Whatever it is you would like to tell me."

"I'm not sure how it would make any difference to you."

"Why wouldn't it make a difference to me?"

"We seem to have these kind of circular conversations, and I find them quite annoying."

"Indulge me," he said.

"Fine. I don't see why you would care because
you're a sheikh. Because you're important. Because you have money and that means other
people rarely matter in a sincere way."

"Is that what you think? It seems a very cyni-
cal way to view the world."

Her cheeks colored, her mouth pulled into a
tightly drawn line. "Hey, I've earned my world-
view, on that you can trust me. I wasn't from
a family with a name anyone recognized. That
made me lesser. So you can see why I feel a lit-

tle bit surprised that someone like you would care to hear about me."

He was happy to use this moment to keep the microscope on her. To keep her in the iron sights of this conversation rather than submitting himself to an examination. "Your surprise is misplaced. Now that you've said all that, I find I'm even more curious." What she was talking about was something that was far outside his experience in many ways. People had always treated him with a certain amount of deference because he was a ruler. Because he had power and, as she had mentioned before, money. However, he also knew far too well that it did not erase all of one's problems.

"There isn't much to be curious about. I grew up in your standard low-end neighborhood. On a small street, with smaller houses. I had a single mother who worked quite a bit, so I was left on my own a lot. But it didn't bother me. It gave me time to study. I decided from a really early age that I wasn't going to settle for the kind of life my mother had."

"It sounds to me like your mother was admirable. Working to keep you fed."

"I don't disrespect that. But my mother had an unhealthy attachment to my father. And I watched it destroy her. I watched it kill any chance she might have had at happiness. She didn't ever want to move because he had bought the house for us. She didn't want to go where he could not easily come and visit. She didn't want to get too invested in a job, because she needed to be able to drop it at a moment's notice if he came for her. He rarely did. And as I got older he stopped coming at all. I swore I would never be that way. I swore that I would be independent. And I knew that the only way I would manage that was by getting an education, and getting a job that could support me. So here I am."

"That is very admirable indeed."

"You don't have to sound so dry about it. It actually *is* admirable. I worked hard. I'm still working hard."

"I didn't mean for it to sound dry." He knew how hard it was to change yourself, how hard it was to break patterns of behavior. He had done it with himself. Though he had not had the type of obstacles she'd had. In fact, all of his obstacles had been self-built. But in the end he knew the sort of thing she was talking about was no simple task.

"Well, then your sincerity is unexpected, and appreciated."

"Very good." They finished their meal, and when they were done he stood. "Would you like to accompany me to my study?"

"I assume there you will discuss business."

"You assume correctly. You answered my questions. Now, I will answer some of yours." He extended his arm, and she looked at it as though he was offering her a lizard. "I will not bite you. I am simply being chivalrous."

"Oh, I'm sorry. I missed it somehow. You know, considering our history together."

"Fair enough." But he kept his arm extended.

She took a step toward him and curled her slender arm through his elbow, her body sliding close to his. And in that moment he knew he had vastly underestimated the dress. Because the moment she touched him he burned. The moment she touched him he thought of nothing but pressing her up against the nearest wall and bringing his mouth down on hers.

It was a wild and errant fantasy. The kind he had not had in more years than he could count.

While he had not given up sex entirely until his engagement had become official, he had given up this. This kind of intense heat. The driving sort of need that transcended everything. From duty and honor to decorum and appropriate behavior for the public. Because once he had her against that wall, once his mouth touched hers, he would be hard-pressed to stop.

He shut down that line of thinking. It would not happen. He would not touch her.

His engagement to Christine would be honored. Though he and his fiancée did not have a physical relationship, they had made an agreement. And he would respect that.

If Samson had had the foresight to stay away from Delilah, he would've been spared quite a bit of trouble. Zayn intended to spare himself the trouble. He would not touch Sophie.

He adjusted his hold on her, disengaging his arm from hers and placing his hand on her lower back. The gesture was provocative, more intimate than the previous one. He was doing it to test himself. Doing it to prove to himself that he was not a slave.

She tensed beneath his touch, but did not look at him. She didn't stop. Perhaps she was testing herself, too.

No, he would not think of that. That way lay madness.

They walked from the dining room, and down the corridor that led to his quarters.

The study was different to the rest of the palace. Most of this portion of it was. Zayn had never moved quarters when his parents had left. Instead choosing to stay in the rooms he had called home from the time he was a child. He had remodeled them as an adult. The study had a more European feel to it. Dark wood bookcases, large windows that overlooked the gardens outside. And armchairs. Places for him to read. When he had given up partying, when he'd given up womanizing, he'd had to find a hobby. Reading seemed as good as any.

"Well, this is different than what I imagined."

"What is it you imagined?" he asked.

"Well, not this."

"I am gratified that I was able to surprise you." He released his hold on her and gestured to one of the velvet armchairs. "Please have a seat."

He took a seat across from her, a healthy amount of space between them. "Would you like something to drink?"

"I feel a brandy is in order."

He chuckled. "A brandy. Yes, naturally." He stood again and made his way over to the bar in the corner of the room, picking up a decanter and pouring both of them a healthy portion of amber liquid. He made his way back over to the chairs, handing her a glass, careful to ensure that his fingers did not brush hers.

He took a seat across from her again.

"Thank you." She swirled the liquid, lifting it to her lips, blinking when it touched her tongue.

"Strong?"

"No. Not strong at all."

"We wouldn't want it going to your head. You have an interview to conduct."

She cleared her throat and straightened, setting the glass on the rich wood side table. "Yes, so…about the Chatsfields."

He waved his hand, silencing her. "No, that is not how we are doing this."

"What?"

"If you want to interview me, it will be on my terms. We will do this my way, or we will not do it at all. We will go back to talking about the very hot weather."

"That isn't how an interview works. I'm not sure if you've ever had one conducted?"

"It is how an interview works with me. If you don't like it, spend the remainder of your time here in your room, and get nothing from me."

"You know, you really are a demanding bastard."

"I have never claimed to be anything else."

"Fair point," she said, her tone dry.

"Your boss wants an article on the wedding. And I think in order for you to get a good picture of the wedding, you need to understand some things about the circumstances my country is in."

"Okay," she answered slowly.

"In order to understand why the marriage is important, you must understand the monarchy."

"I was always a very good study in world history. I do know some things about Surhaadi."

He leaned back in his chair, a smile curving his lips. "Really? Do enlighten me on all of your knowledge of my country."

"I didn't mean to sound all arrogant about it. It's only that I am somewhat familiar."

"Yes, well, you may be somewhat familiar, but it is in my blood. The history of Surhaadi is a part of me, like flesh over bone."

She reached down and picked up her purse, pulling out a small black device. "Tape recorder."

He inclined his head. "Of course."

It stood to reason that she would be recording their interactions, for ease when she compiled the conversations into an article. But it also made him conscious of the fact that he would have to be very careful in what he told her. She would have his words recorded, and she would be able to play them back, turn them over. Dissect them for meaning.

He continued. "But, of course, before you can understand the monarchy, you must understand how it was founded."

"If you insist."

He could tell that she was quite annoyed with him. Quite annoyed at being subjected to a history lesson rather than simply being handed the information she was after. But he had to keep her here, and he was busily trying to construct a way to do that. To keep her hanging out for information that he did not have, so that she would remain of her own accord. There was little honor in this kind of behavior, but he had given up any chances of being truly honorable years ago. He could hardly grieve the loss of it now. He could only afford it where the treatment of his family was concerned. And nowhere else.

In actuality, he had no intention of throwing her in a dungeon. And were she to escape the palace there was a limit to what he could do. Certainly, he was the sheikh, but he could hardly have a woman going to the media and claiming he had kidnapped her, and was holding her in the palace. Which meant that if she escaped he could not go after her. In which case she would simply be written off as a spurned lover. Or a woman who had been spurned in an attempt to be his lover.

That his reputation could transcend. The kidnapping very likely not.

"I do insist."

"Okay, then let's start at the beginning." She leaned back in her chair, her hand poised on the record button.

"My family has been in Surhaadi for at least a thousand years. Of course, at the time it was not one unified kingdom. Rather, it was a territory populated by a series of independently ruled tribes." This was like reciting remedial history, and he'd never paid much attention to history in school, but as an adult he had started to appreciate his country's past. Had started investigating it on his own.

Another hobby he'd started after giving up partying.

"The desert is large, and so there is ample access to territory, but what there is not ample access to is water. The need for water, the need for plants to graze animals, the need for food, occasionally caused battles to break out among the tribes. As the landscape changed, water became more scarce. And it came to a point where a specific tribe refused to move away from an oasis. Refused to allow others passage to water. That was when my people knew changes had to be made. There was a call for unification. If only temporarily so that the people could have food. Could have the water they needed. So that they could band together and deal with the threat facing their lives."

"When was this?"

"About three hundred years ago. As kingdoms go we aren't an old one." He could see that in spite of herself she was interested. He found it gratifying that she might be. Because for all that he had scorned the traditions of his country in his youth, as a man the pulse of the desert ran through his blood. It was a part of him, as was each and every soul that populated the kingdom. "The tribes banded together, and due to their increase in number they not only successfully regained control of the oasis, they were able to do so without starting a war. This led to the desire for further change. Concern over outside threats brought a call for more permanent unity."

"So they decided to form one nation?"

"Eventually. Even though there were, of course, some issues. And the tribe that was defeated at the oasis declined to join."

"And now? Have they moved? Have they joined?"

"They still live in Surhaadi. And they still claim independence from the monarchy. Though we do have some hand in their lives. They have the option to partake in various government programs, though for the most part they decline. They are broken into several different groups now, and live most of the year away from the city deep in the desert."

"And you don't have any issues with them?"

"Not as such. Though the leaders are not overly friendly. They see me as a challenge to their authority, and my authority is not readily recognized within the borders of their territory."

"But you aren't afraid of them? You haven't seen the need to draw them into the fold, so to speak."

"I see no need to destroy centuries worth of culture in a power grab. A treaty was signed long ago between their family and mine. As long as we do not interfere with them to their detriment, they will not interfere with us. And if we are in need, we are allowed use of any oasis we might find in their territory."

"That seems fair enough. But how did your family find itself being selected as the ruling family?"

He placed his glass back down on the table. "That, I think, is a story for another night."

"You seem to fundamentally misunderstand your function in an interview."

"It seems to me that you should be exhausted from the trip."

"I slept on the plane."

"Hours ago. And if you do not get on schedule here in Surhaadi as quickly as possible, your jet lag will be fierce."

"I've never been in a position where I might be jet-lagged. So I have no idea what it's like."

"It's a bit like being hungover."

She blinked. "Well, I've never been hungover before, either."

"How is that possible?"

"You aren't the only person who prizes a bit of control."

Suddenly, she seemed even more intriguing than she had before. "You must have quite a bit of control in your possession, then."

"People like me do not have power bestowed upon them from birth. We have to find it in ourselves. We have to take it where we can. In my case, that meant seizing control over my own life. Over my own behavior. It never mattered to me what my contemporaries did. It only ever mattered what I did."

"Admirable."

"I don't know if it's admirable. I don't particularly care if it's admirable. But it has worked for me. At least up until the moment when I got pulled out of an alleyway in New York City."

"Yes, I would apologize for that, but I'm not sorry."

"I didn't think you were."

"I appreciate the exchange of information—" he inclined his head "—it has been very informative."

Her cheeks blushed rose. "Is that what we're doing? Exchanging information?"

"It seems fair, doesn't it?"

"Not particularly. I didn't think that was part of our deal. I interview you, you tell me about the Chatsfields."

Technically, he had not said that. Technically, all he had promised her was a scandal. But he would not correct her, not now. "Instant gratification can be damaging. I believe in working for what you want."

"That's rich coming from a man who was undoubtedly born with a golden scepter in his hand."

She was not wrong, for many things in his life had been delivered to him at the snap of his fingers. But that had been a contributing factor in forming the man he had become. And the man he had been was not one he could be proud of. It had taken hardship to change him.

"It's true. I cannot deny it. I have also suffered. And no amount of money could insulate me from that suffering. I've learned that sometimes you simply have no choice but to walk through the fire. And if you come out the other side, then the reward is great."

"Are you my trial by fire?" she asked.

"Perhaps one of them. I wouldn't presume to know if you'd had others or not."

"I appreciate that. I'm sure you've suffered greatly here in your palace. But I am no stranger to suffering. I'm also no stranger to hard work, so trust me when I tell you you're preaching to the choir. Though, also, forgive me for saying I'm a bit jaded to the concept that hard work somehow makes something more rewarding. I've put in more hard work to get where I am than many people ever will. I find it more exhausting than rewarding. There were some times when I would've simply rather had the playing field even, rather than subjecting myself to character-building exercises. It is easy to romanticize what we've never had to endure."

He almost laughed at the irony of the statement. He looked around the ornate room. "Indeed."

"I suppose I should take my leave. I might need a map of this place, if you have one handy, otherwise I fear I will spend a good portion of my time wandering around feeling lost."

"I have a feeling it would be best for me if you felt a little bit lost. In which case, you would cause me less trouble."

"Don't bet on that. I imagine I will contrive new ways to cause you trouble daily. Until I get what I want."

"What is it you want?" he asked, knowing what her answer would be.

"What is it you're hiding?" she asked.

The question took him off guard. Perhaps because she had grazed far too close to the bone.

Not just in terms of Leila.

"Nothing but the usual skeletons," he managed, knowing his voice sounded strangled, affected.

"I look forward to seeing them," she said.

He gritted his teeth. "I am not James Chatsfield." Neither did he actually have any information on Chatsfield he could share.

"I know," she said, nodding once.

If he had thought he'd understood her, he'd been wrong. Bitterly so. She'd put him on his back foot, and he didn't like it. For one thing, she was far too beautiful. For another, she was unpredictable. "Excellent. And on that note, I bid you good-night. My quarters are just here, so you will forgive me if I do not walk you back to yours. It is quite a trek." And he had a feeling, that were he to accompany her in dark corridors, his control would be tested in ways he did not want to think of.

"I shall manage. Though if I end up in a royal vault and decide to abscond with the crown jewels, you will have no one to blame but yourself."

"It is a risk I shall have to take."

"Clearly you're a man who lives on the edge."

Her words brought them up short. "On that score you would be wrong." He nodded firmly, turning away from her, breaking the connection between them. The sooner he got rid of her, the better. "Good night."

Behind him he heard her voice, slightly shaken,

confused. He did not care, or rather, he should not. "Good night."

Her tone of voice made him want to speak again. Made him want to say something kinder, something not quite so short and harsh.

"Later this week I shall take you to see the desert…"

He did not know why he was offering this, except that it was a chance to show the world what Surhaadi was, who they were. And she had seemed interested.

Moreover, he needed to keep her busy. He could not have her wandering about the palace appearing to be a lover, or a captive. Not considering the fact that media attention would be on them very soon for the wedding, not considering that he had a fiancée he had made certain he was faithful to.

If he had a story to give his staff, things would be better. Yes, she was a reporter covering the wedding and the history of Surhaadi.

Yes, getting her out of the palace for the day would be the best course of action. Taking her out to see the Bedouin tribe would be good, seeing as it would give her something to focus on that had nothing to do with Leila or James Chatsfield.

"And after that?" She was fishing for the scandal, still. She was right, she was rather stubborn.

"After that we will continue the interview."

"And I will have my scandal?"

"You will have your scandal."

And with that, he strode from the room, without looking back.

CHAPTER FIVE

ZAYN MANAGED TO avoid her for the next several days, setting a firm departure time for their trip to the desert late in the week.

She spent those days rattling around the palace, feeling slightly shaky and deprived since she had no contact with the outside world. She was ready to trade her kingdom for some internet. Or Zayn's, since she didn't actually have a kingdom.

The day of their desert trek dawned bright and early. She'd lost some sense of time and place after being cooped up in the palace, but still she was up, and dressed, courtesy of the clothing that had been provided for her by Zayn. It was a strange thing, having an entirely new wardrobe just sitting there for her. Not so idly she wondered if she would be able to bring it home with her. Then she felt guilty for wondering about that. But it wasn't as though she could afford to go refresh her wardrobe every season, or even every year. And as projecting a polished, professional image was important in her line of work, she knew the clothing was important, too. And, as always, she was conscious of the fact that she was working from a disadvantaged place. People were more likely to be watching for her to appear low class, disheveled or cheap. Because once they knew where she came from they expected those things.

Isabelle could go to work in sweatpants and it would be assumed she was on the cutting edge of some fashion statement. The same consideration would not be given to Sophie. Not that either of them would ever go to work in sweatpants. For all that Isabelle had many advantages due to her name, she never seemed to take them for granted. Neither did she seem to rest on her laurels. It was just another reason why the two had become fast friends in spite of their differences.

And as she wandered through the corridor, wondering where she was supposed to meet Zayn, her thoughts turned back to why she was here.

She took a deep breath, and adjusted the loose, flowing tunic top she was wearing. She had a mission, and she would do well to remember that.

The interview she'd conducted earlier in the

week had been informative, and certainly held information she could use in the piece she would write for the *Herald*. But it had not furthered her cause where Isabelle was concerned. And she could not allow herself to be too distracted.

Nevertheless, she was excited to get out of the palace and see some of the countryside. This was her first experience with world travel, with seeing a culture that was different from her own, that wasn't just confined to a few blocks somewhere in New York City.

She walked into the entryway of the palace and stopped in her tracks when she saw Zayn standing there. He was dressed in a tunic and light pants, similar to her own, a headdress covering his dark hair. He had a length of fabric in his hands, strong brown fingers curved tightly around it.

"It is hot today, and there will be a lot of wind as we head away from the city. This will help."

He held the fabric out to her and she approached slowly. "We won't get caught in a sandstorm or anything like that, will we?" she asked.

The little she knew about weather in the desert was that it could be unpredictable, and very harsh.

"It can be a risk. Sandstorms hit hard and without warning when they come. Sometimes there are floods to contend with, but those at least come with warning. But we do have state-of-the-art transportation, and if things get bad before we leave the encampment, we will be cared for there."

"So, we're actually going to visit the people who refused to become part of Surhaadi as a nation?"

"Yes, but as I said, while they do not like to give me too much deference, for obvious reasons, we are quite friendly with each other. And they will not let me die out in the middle of the sands. At least, I hope not."

"Your confidence astounds." She accepted the scarf from him and surreptitiously studied the way he had draped his own over his head. She did her best to try and copy the fashion. She hated asking for help more than just about anything. She always wanted to step right in, and pick something up by observation. Never revealing the fact that she didn't simply arrive knowing how things work.

That stubbornness again, and yes, a bit of misplaced pride. But it came with a lot of long-held anger over what might have been. That if her father weren't a philanderer, or if he were at least honest about the fact that he was, she might have been treated like a child, and not a dirty secret. That if she'd been part of her family, raised in that glittering home upstate, she would have absorbed social graces, would have known how to navigate university and different social situations. Instead, she'd had to conduct herself with trial and error, and she had learned to fear the error.

So she had observed those around her, painstakingly so, in order to look as though she belonged. She hated asking for help. Hated admitting her shortcomings.

"Let me help you." He took a step closer to her, and she took a step back.

"I have it." She knew she was being stubborn, she didn't care.

"You do not." He extended his hands, and gripped the fabric, adjusting it where it sat on her head, drawing a swath of it around and bringing it beneath her chin before tucking it into the folds of fabric at the base of her neck.

His thumb brushed against her jaw, the heat from his skin a shock to her system. She looked up, her eyes crashing into his. The expression she found there intense, dark, hinting at things she could scarcely understand. She wondered if he always operated at this level of intensity, or if it was something about her. If he was reacting to the touch, in the same way she had.

She should look away, and she knew it. She should pretend that this hadn't happened.

That he had touched her, but that it hadn't registered as anything. But she couldn't look away, she couldn't pretend. Because something about his gaze held her fast, something about it called her, tugged at something deep inside of her that had been previously unknown, previously untouched. And it didn't matter how much she wanted to ignore it, because her body simply wouldn't let her.

And she found she still couldn't look away.

She needed to. Oh, Lord, she needed to. This dark, yawning chasm that opened up in her stomach when he looked at her had to be covered up and never looked in. Never examined.

The idea that his could be attraction was unthinkable. That she could find herself interested in a man who was so far above her, who was engaged...

It would make her no better than her mother. And she could never allow that to happen.

Not to mention the fact that she should hate him on principle for forcing her hand and bringing her here.

Why was it so hard to hate him?

He cleared his throat and straightened. "There, that is more secure. You will find you have better protection against the elements."

"I appreciate that." It sounded so insipid, so forced, and she had a feeling he knew it. But it was the best she could do. Because her throat had gone drier than the desert sand outside, and all of her words seemed intent on sticking to it.

"I do strive to be of service to those who are in my country." His voice was rough, yet smooth at the same time, like velvet. It slid over her skin, leaving a strange sensation behind, causing goose bumps to rise up on her arms.

"Well, given the fact that I am currently in your country for an unforeseeable amount of time, I do take that as a comfort."

"I'm glad."

"I suppose we should leave?" She had no idea if they should leave, if they were on any kind of timeline at all, but anything seemed better than standing here in the entryway feeling like the tile was shifting beneath her feet, feeling like she might die of heatstroke in spite of the cool air around them.

"Certainly." He turned sharply and headed toward the double doors, which opened when he approached. She followed him closely, blinking against the harsh light as they stepped outside.

There was a large SUV parked near the doors. There was no driver, which surprised her.

"We aren't going by ourselves, are we?"

"I am very familiar with the terrain, it shall be fine."

For some reason she couldn't quantify, his driving skills were not the concern. It was the idea of being alone with him. Even the other night in the study, though it had felt isolated, she had been aware of the fact that there were still people around them.

"Why are we going alone?"

"So as not to look like a descending army. I do all my business with Jamal and his people alone."

"You're not taking me out to the desert to kill me."

"Don't be absurd. If I was going to do such a thing, I would simply leave you to die. I wouldn't do anything so prosaic as *killing* you."

"Color me relieved. I don't suppose you would joke about leaving me out in the desert to die if that were actually your plan."

"It is very difficult to say." He opened the passenger door and held it for her.

She looked at him hard. He was impossible to read, but she didn't imagine that the man who had just so carefully adjusted her veil so that she might be protected against the elements could have any intention of leaving her out in the middle of the desert. No point in making her comfortable only to let her die of heatstroke.

With that in mind, she got into the car, but

kept her eyes on him as he closed the door behind her. He rounded the front of the vehicle and got in, buckling his seat belt and putting the car in gear. She hurried to buckle, as well.

"How long does it take to get there?"

He flashed her a smile, his teeth bright against his dark skin, and she realized it was the first time she had ever seen a genuine smile on his face. "That all depends on where we might find them today."

They drove for ages, until the road faded, until the sand rose higher, turning a richer golden brown, as though the sun were closer here, baking it like bread. And in spite of the care that Zayn had taken with her head covering earlier, she was starting to get worried again about the possibility of him leaving her out in the middle of nowhere. Paranoid, possibly, but she supposed not entirely without merit, seeing as he had already brought her to his country by force. Well, partial force, partial bribery. She still wasn't certain whether or not he would've chased her if she had tried to run off, but she would've found herself jobless, and that was threat enough.

Just when she was starting to get truly nervous, she saw a spiral of smoke rising up from behind a dune.

"That would be them." Zayn's deep voice answered the question she hadn't even been able to ask yet.

"They really are quite a ways out here. What happens if there's some kind of medical emergency?"

"Often it isn't a happy ending. Though now they have satellite phones, and they do often use the rescue services available in Surhaadi."

"They use the medical services, even though they don't acknowledge the government?"

"Most of the time. Though there are some elders who refuse to do so. I prefer that they do."

"That's very decent of you. I think there are a lot of leaders who wouldn't like that. Who would say that it was the cost of their stubbornness."

She looked over at him, at his strong profile, his eyes fixed on the horizon. "Yes, I suppose that is the case. But then, we all make decisions, often they are not wholly bad, but not wholly good, either. They want to preserve their heritage, and I understand that. And then, when tragedy strikes, often it becomes apparent that remaining separate can cause damage. But there is no real right or wrong answer in this. And I do not fault them for wanting help when they are desperate. I know what it's like to change because of circumstances. I know what it's like to see the error of your ways when it's too late."

This was a different side of him, the strong ruler versus the modern-day marauder who had taken her from New York. The man who served an entire populace, not just his family. This was the history of his country personified, and she could see now why he had wanted her to come out here.

The car maneuvered slowly over the top of the dune, and the encampment came into view. Nestled on the edge of an oasis that had been invisible until this very moment. The sun shone on the water, the still surface reflected everything like a mirror. Tents were erected along the embankment, children running in circles around them. There were cooking fires already started, clothes hanging across lines, blowing in the breeze.

"I'm hoping we'll receive a warm welcome."

"Do you think there's a chance we won't?" she asked.

"I never take anything for granted, especially out here. Because out here, it does not matter that I am the sheikh. Not to them, and not to the desert. We are simply guests, myself as much as you. Though they are familiar with me."

He brought the car to a stop, and turned the

engine off. They were still a great distance away from the encampment, but she imagined this was part of not seeming as though he was storming the camp.

He got out and she followed suit, her feet sinking into the sand. She adjusted her weight, and shook the remaining sand out of her pant leg. "You almost need snowshoes to walk on this."

"Or practice," he said.

"Don't sound so amused. I don't often make a habit of going to the beach, but this is kind of an extreme version of that. And I'm unpracticed as it is."

"Too late, *habibti*, I am amused. It cannot be helped."

"Perhaps I should simply slide down the dune, and make a grand entrance."

"I would prefer if you did not. But I am not in total control of your actions, neither do I pretend to be."

She laughed. "Oh, that's rich. I think you fancy yourself entirely in control of my actions."

"I am not so foolish as to think that I could control you entirely."

She shook her head, her hair hemmed in by the head covering. "Good. I would hate for you to be so deceived. Because as we discussed previously, I am nothing if not determined."

"I believe the word you used earlier was *stubborn*."

"They're the same, aren't they?"

"I imagine for the purposes of dealing with you, they are about the same."

"I'm flattered to hear you say that."

She would've liked nothing more than to walk on ahead of him, gliding gracefully over the surface of the sand, but for several reasons that wasn't going to happen. One, because she was incapable of gliding across the surface of the sand, and two, because she was not going into the encampment alone.

Fortunately, Zayn took the lead, and she was able to follow behind him. It all felt very medieval, her walking in his shadow. But then, in the moment, there was very little she could do about it.

She was quite annoyed to see that he had no issues walking across the sand at all. It made her feel clunky, it made her feel disadvantaged. And she hated all of that. Yes, it was a little bit silly to be worrying about it out here in the middle of nowhere. To be worried about the fact that she looked so out of place, but it was ingrained in her that that was a bad thing, and she could hardly change her feelings on the subject now.

When they got to the bottom of the dune, he

paused, and turned back to face her. "Wait here. I'm going to go forward and see if they are in a mind to receive visitors, and I do not want you near me just in case."

"Just in case what?

"As I said, I don't take anything in the desert for granted."

She watched Zayn walk ahead, fear tightening her stomach and she wasn't sure why. For herself, obviously. But then, she could always make a run for the dune, and for the vehicle. But she feared that it wasn't only concern for herself that had her feeling on edge. But concern for Zayn. And he did not deserve her concern, all things considered.

But it was hard to wish the loss of a ruler on a nation, especially when the ruler appeared to be as caring as Zayn was. Yes, on a personal level she had found him difficult to deal with, but whenever he spoke of his country, whenever he spoke of his people, he seemed ideal. He was even willing to marry to further things for his people, and how could she fault him for that?

How could a nation ask for a stronger leader? For one who was willing to sacrifice himself on a greater level? Was there a greater level other than death to sacrifice yourself on? She doubted it.

So, that was why she was nervous. It had

nothing to do with the way she felt about him, because all she felt for him was annoyance. Simple as.

He approached the edge of the encampment and stood, his hands outstretched, proving that he had no weapons, or at least that was what Sophie imagined he was doing. It was very possible that she was getting a bit overdramatic.

Overdramatic or not, she watched with bated breath, unsure of what might happen next. She wished he had brought some kind of protection with him because on this score she would be of no use to him. All she could do was plot her own escape. Which would be foiled by her inability to move quickly in the terrain. She might as well go out with honor.

Suddenly the man Zayn was talking to pulled him into an embrace. When they parted, Zayn looked back at Sophie, then started to walk her direction. His dark eyes were locked with hers and her stomach tightened in response. She did her best to school her expression into one of neutrality, but she wasn't sure if she was quite managing it. Because he threw her off, darn it. Of course, who could blame her? He had brought her out to the middle of the desert and then had, in no uncertain terms, told her that their reception might be less than warm.

And then he had left her standing on top of the dune. Yes, it wasn't him that was throwing her off. It was the situation.

Then he moved closer, his dark eyes trained on hers, and a shiver worked its way down her spine. It was a lot harder, in that moment, to pretend the fear had been entirely for her.

"We are welcome," Zayn said.

"Well, that's good. I was already mentally planning on how I would relay your valiant fight to save yourself to your staff when I returned back in the SUV without you."

She took a step toward him and stumbled. The wry smile that curved his lips said everything his voice didn't. She was not running anywhere out here, and they both knew it. Not when she could scarcely walk a few steps without nearly falling on her face.

"I even explained to Jamal that you are a reporter. He still didn't kick us out. I think that's a good sign."

"So he doesn't mind me making observations that will end up in the news?"

"They remain fairly unaffected by world events out here, but that isn't to say it doesn't matter. As long as your representation is fair, he will not mind. Though I have to say I'm surprised that you care one way or the other."

Heat stung Sophie's face, and it wasn't just

from the sun. "Look, you've made some assumptions about me based on what you think a reporter is, and based on the fact that you think I'm basically a tabloid journalist, and given what I was up to when we met I can't really blame you. But I write for the society pages for the *New York Herald* and that's a far cry from the tabloids. Also, I'm a human being with feelings, and I acknowledge that other human beings have feelings. I'm not out to destroy anybody."

"Except for the Chatsfields."

She cleared her throat. "I never said I wanted to destroy them. I merely want to distract them."

"To what end?"

"If you get to keep your secrets, then I get to keep mine. Now, rather than keeping me standing out here in the middle of the sand, why don't you introduce me to your friend?"

"*Friend* is used loosely here." Zayn moved to her side, and put his hand on her lower back, guiding her in the direction of the man he had called Jamal.

The man was tall, nearly the same height as Zayn, his expression even more imposing. "You must be the reporter," he said.

"Yes, that's me." She extended her hand, only to find it ignored. She put it awkwardly back at her side, wobbling a bit on the uneven sand. "Sophie. Sophie Parsons."

The man nodded his head. "I suppose then we should give you something interesting to report on."

CHAPTER SIX

"WE HAVE SENT your woman back to the tent."

Zayn looked at Jamal, something strange twisting in his gut as he turned over the words the other man had just spoken. "She is merely under my protection. Nothing more."

"Then would you prefer she sleep elsewhere?"

"As I said," Zayn replied, knowing he should be taking Jamal up on his offer, knowing he wouldn't, "she is under my protection. That means she must stay close with me."

"As you wish."

"There is nothing between us."

Jamal looked off into the distance, his eyes fixed on the horizon line. "It is none of my concern what you do or with whom. I care not for your affairs, Al-Ahmar. You should know this by now. So long as you stay out of my business, I will stay out of yours."

"To a point, I'm certain."

"Well, you are here now. So obviously it only

extends to a point. Though I will say it is lucky for you that you now have me to deal with rather than my father. His welcome for you may not have been so hospitable."

"And yet, hostility between us is pointless. We both want the same things. We both want what is absolutely best for those we rule over."

"Ah, yes. But I do believe you and I often have differing opinions on what is best."

Zayn looked toward the tent that was being provided for Sophie and himself. "I sometimes differ with myself as to what is best."

"Indeed." Jamal laughed. "Don't we all?"

Far too often. "I shall retire now."

Jamal arched a brow. "As would I if I had a woman such as that waiting for me in my tent."

"*You* have a wife. And this woman is not my lover."

"Calm down, Al-Ahmar. I have no designs on your woman. Neither will I repeat what I have seen here. We may not agree on everything, but I believe you are a man of honor. And for that reason I do not see the point in causing you any trouble."

Zayn extended his hand, and Jamal clasped it and shook it. "On that we agree. And I must bid you good-night now."

He turned and walked away from the other man, ignoring his assumptions. Doing his best to push them away from his mind. Yes, he and Sophie would share a tent tonight. But there was plenty of room for both of them. And he would not touch her.

He crossed the courtyard, passing the campfires that were starting to die down. He swept up the closure of the tent and encountered a wide-eyed-looking Sophie.

"Good evening." He turned away from her and continued on to the corner of the massive space, where there was a seating area, where the bags he had had his staff prepare for them were sitting.

"What are you doing here?"

"This is a guest quarters. And as we are both guests, this is where we will both be staying."

"I don't even have any…" Her sentence trailed off as she looked at the bags he was now standing next to.

"You have everything. Naturally."

"Naturally. I'm beginning to discover that staying with you means being taken care of whether I want to be or not." He only stared at her. "Well, that's not what I mean exactly."

"You mean I give you absolutely no excuses for being unhappy? I make you comfortable. It must be awful considering you're trying to feel like the wounded prisoner."

"Well, I do feel slightly like the *invaded* prisoner at the moment. I was not aware we would be sharing a tent."

He swept his hand across the expanse of the vast space. "Did you think you would have such a place to yourself?"

She blinked, tossing golden hair over her shoulders, the strands turning to golden fire in the lantern light. "I confess I didn't really think it through."

"I don't suppose you did." He gestured toward a swath of silk that was suspended from the ceiling. "Back there you will find the bed. It is fine with me if you have it. I'm happy to sleep on the couch."

"As long as you acknowledge we're sleeping in separate places." He watched as her cheeks turned a fascinating shade of pink after the words left her lips.

"Naturally." He jerked up the zipper on the duffel bag sitting on the couch, only to discover that it was the bag that had been filled with Sophie's clothes. His hands came into contact with silk, smooth and slick, and not what he needed right at the moment. "I am not in the market for a lover. And were I in the market for a lover, it would certainly not be you."

She sniffed. "Good. As long as we have an understanding."

"Yes, as long as we do." Heat burned in his

chest, and his palms burned from where he had just made contact with the feminine clothing. Three years of celibacy really was far too long. If women's clothing had the ability to get him hard, it was obvious things had been left untended for way too much time.

"Changing topic completely," she said, "I think it's time for the second part of our interview."

"Do you think so?"

She crossed the space and moved to the sitting area, to the low chaise that sat across from the couch he was currently standing next to. She sat on the chaise, leaning against the back, the position accentuating her shape, forcing his eyes to her curves.

He shoved the duffel bags onto the floor and took a seat across from her. "I fear tonight there is no alcohol to help make this process any less painful."

"I'm okay with that. I don't actually drink all that much." She propped her cheek on her fist.

"Why is that?"

"High in calories, expensive. Compromises control."

"Yes, so you said. When you mentioned you had never had a hangover."

She reached into the pocket of her pants and produced the little black recorder again. "You seem to be forgetting who's doing the interviewing again."

"No, I never forget. But I never give without getting in return. It is simply not how I operate."

"And I don't like to talk about myself. And you keep forcing the situation so that I am. It's very irritating."

"My apologies."

"I doubt I have any sincere apologies from you. So let's continue, shall we?"

He abruptly changed his mind about sitting. And pushed himself back to his feet. "What was it you asked me the other night?"

"I asked how it was your family ended up being in power. How are they chosen? I'm curious about the history of the Al-Ahmar family."

"Yes." He remembered, of course, but he had wanted her to bring it up again. Had wanted her to feel as though she was directing the flow of the interview. "Yes, that's right. That is what you asked. As with anything, changes are imperfect. There was a time when we all lived like this." He swept his hand around the tent. "Of course, we had no satellite phones."

"Naturally not."

"When we banded together, it was natural to want to come together under one leader. It was what we were used to."

"You talk about it like you were there."

He shrugged his shoulders. He supposed he did. Though it was something he barely gave any thought to. This was his history. "In many ways I was. My bloodline was there. It is not my direct family line that rules now, though we are the blood ancestors of the tribe that ended up taking control. It is a part of me."

She shifted her position, and he turned away. "I'm curious, though, what it was that singled your people out as being worthy of leadership."

"Do not think it wasn't highly contested. It was no unanimous vote that brought my bloodline into power. But when war with a neighboring country broke out, a country that had long been unified especially in comparison with ours, it was my people who proved to be the greatest warriors. And it was in fact the death of our tribal leader in that battle, saving the women and children of another tribal group, that decided it. He would have been king, he would have been the sheikh, but he had perished protecting others. And so his son was made the first ruler of what became known as Surhaadi."

Silence fell between them. There was no sound beyond the wind pushing against the tent.

"What a sad story. He sacrificed himself and he never knew what it accomplished."

He turned back to her. "I like to think he knew. Whether or not he ever knew that it accomplished installing our family as the ruling power, I like to believe he knew in the end his sacrifice saved the women and children he set out to protect. He fought until he could not move, destroyed enemies, removed every threat, before breathing his last. I like to think he knew the most important thing his sacrifice accomplished."

She looked away. "Well, it's certainly a better ending. Even if you can't quite call it a happier ending."

"I like to think his sacrifice established what kind of leaders the Al-Ahmar family became. It is certainly the unspoken covenant that was made. That whoever should take charge of the newly banded-together tribes would lay down his life to protect the weakest among them. That he would not love his own life so much that he would seek protection for himself over others."

She sat up, her hands folded in her lap, the recorder clutched in one of them. "Do you feel you do that? Do you feel you are carrying on the tradition?"

"Do I feel I am as self-sacrificial as an ancestor of mine who physically died protecting those around him? No. I don't. However, I have done what I can to make sacrifices when I can, where I can."

"Your marriage?"

He hesitated. This was on the record, this was an interview. One that would go out to millions of people worldwide. And as Sophie had already mentioned, the public loved a love story. But beyond that, he had no desire to hurt Christine with unvarnished honesty. That was assuming, of course, that Christine could be hurt by honesty, and he had doubts that she could be. But even so, sensitivity was very likely the better part of valor in this situation. Too bad he had not often been accused of being overly sensitive.

"I have always known that I would marry. For many years I had known it would be Christine. Ours is not a traditional relationship. We have not spent much time together, it is not physical. But it *is* based on love. A love for our countries. A desire to see things improve. If you see parallels there in terms of sacrifice, that is up to you."

She leaned forward, green eyes intent on his. "Do you feel the love of a country is enough?"

"It is the truest love I know. It runs through my veins."

"And you do not believe in love between two people?"

He had not picked her for a romantic, and indeed, there was only curiosity in her tone now. But still, there was something beneath it, something that fascinated him. Something that made him ache.

He thought of his own parents' cold, distant union. And then he thought of Jasmine and her lover. Jasmine and that despicable playboy Damien, who he had once called a friend. Had that been love? An emotion so strong it pushed you to alienate friends and family and make fatal decisions? No, he had never seen evidence of love in his life.

"I am certain such a thing exists—" except that he wasn't, but he was being recorded "—however, for my purposes this is the more lasting. This is more important."

"Have you always felt that way?"

"No," he said, an honest answer slipping from his lips before he could stop it.

"When did it change?"

He froze, his blood turning to ice. "Some time ago."

"Was there a specific event?"

He gritted his teeth, feeling like she'd skillfully led him into a corner. Either he answered with some measure of honesty, or he refused. Refusal, at this point, would only make things worse.

"There used to be three of us. Myself, Jasmine and Leila. Jasmine passed away some years ago," he said, trying to block the images from his mind that always came when he thought of Jasmine. Trying to forget the yelling, the accusations... "Grief like that, loss like that...changes you. It makes you reevaluate."

"I'm sorry," she said. "For your loss."

"It was a long time ago. But it changed things. For all of us."

"Naturally. And anyway, in many ways your life is entirely different to the average person's."

"What do you mean?"

She brushed a strand of blond hair out of her face, and his gaze was caught by the elegant motion of her fingers. The action pulled his thoughts from the past, tugged him out of the mire of it before it could claim him completely.

She was all fine-boned sophistication, and yet there was more to her than that. Something deeper, something grittier and stronger. Were she only softness, were she only grace and poise, he would not be so captivated. It was the strength beneath it, the contrast, that held him in thrall.

"In my life I've only ever had to worry about myself for the most part. I mean, I certainly worry about what other people think of me, make no mistake. But only as it pertains to the way it affects me. You have to do things for other reasons. For bigger reasons. Your whole life is proof positive of the butterfly effect. When you make a small movement it really does affect millions. And I don't think most of us can say that."

"I don't know. You're a journalist. There is information you could bring the world that could easily affect millions. Or at least change the way they think about things." He relished the chance to turn the spotlight back on her. To stop her from shining light on the dark places in his own life.

"That's the ultimate goal. Although I never really thought of it in terms of what I did changing things for other people."

"Did you not?"

"No, I thought about changing things for me. Because the minute I'm done making coffee and doing fluff pieces, I'm sure I'll be able to see changes happening in my own life. Maybe being able to afford a nice new outfit for work. Not having to worry about paying my rent on time. Just being able to rest in the fact that I've made it." She looked like she was about to say something else, her full lips twitching as though something uncomfortable was hovering over them.

"What?"

"It's nothing."

"It is something, or you would not look so much like holding it back was threatening to make you burst." He knew it, because he'd felt it only moments ago.

She shook her head. "I want to reach a point

where I will be admitted into certain functions. And when I am, I will walk up to my father and I will hold out my hand and I will say, 'My name is Sophie Parsons. I don't have your name because I wasn't good enough for you to give it to me. But I'm here now in the same room you are, and whether you like it or not, and whether you want to acknowledge it or not, I am your daughter.'" She blinked rapidly. "And I will tell him that I made it into that room on my own merit. Without his help. Without his name, which is something none of his other children did. I will tell him that the child that wasn't good enough for him is the one who really made it the farthest."

Her words hit him with the force of a punch. In them he could hear where her determination came from. In them he gathered her motivation. And he suddenly understood why she worked so hard to fit in, why she had worked so hard to bring herself up from her modest background.

And it made sense suddenly why she had spoken of her mother with such disdain. It sounded as though the woman had loved someone who had abandoned them entirely, a man who had had other children while refusing to acknowledge her.

It was nothing he could relate to. His place in life had been assured from birth. His blood had assured him entry. His family name a given. A name that stretched back hundreds of years, that brought him reputation, that brought him admiration.

It had been a reputation he hadn't been deserving of for a great many years, one he was striving to deserve now.

And in contrast, the woman across from him had been given nothing in terms of name and reputation. The woman sitting across from him had had to make her own way entirely. If he'd had to do that he would've never been able to transcend the mistakes of his past. But as it was, he had been forgiven. Simply a rebellious wayward royal who'd had too much power, and too much money. A young man who had been far too handsome for his own good, and who had only taken advantage of all that had been naturally afforded him as a result.

He'd had none of her disadvantages, and he'd abused every advantage he *had* been given.

He felt like saying something to her, and yet he felt advice from him was empty. Still, she had shared with him, and he owed something.

"They say the best revenge is living well," he said. "And I feel you are doing that already."

"You can't deny the fact that I'm staying with royalty. Although not so much right now."

"Jamal is royalty in his own right."

"True."

"But in all sincerity, I think your father was a fool. I think he was a fool to deny a daughter such as you."

"Are you complimenting me?" She blinked owlishly.

"Do not seem so surprised. I have admiration for your determination and your mind, even if I cannot leave you entirely to your own devices. I was born with privilege. I was born belonging to my family. And I squandered it. I did not deserve it. It was something I took for granted. I would not be surprised if your other siblings have done the same. Someone like you, a daughter like you, should be appreciated. He did not, and so I think he is a fool."

"How is it that you abused what you were given?" she asked, her voice muted. Her question sounded much more genuine than questions from her did typically. Much more personal, and much less like she was asking as a reporter.

"That I think we will save for tomorrow."

"That doesn't seem fair. And we still didn't get to my scandal."

"We're getting there." His stomach sank as he said the words, as he realized the truth in them. They were getting to the scandal, and he was starting to realize what he would have to give her as substitution for his lack of knowledge about James Chatsfield. As a substitution for the secret his sister carried. The one he had to keep Sophie away from at all costs.

He realized now where his stories were leading her, where they were leading them both. He had not before this moment, but he did now. The founding of a nation, self-sacrifice being the cornerstone of the monarchy. And the importance of acting with honor above all else. Of being worthy of the birthright he had been given without having to do any work at all.

"For tonight I suggest we get some sleep," he said.

She stood, and he stopped pacing, pausing to look at her. The glowing of the lanterns overhead was more pronounced now that the light had dimmed further outside, and it was casting a golden sheen over her. And suddenly everything seemed to narrow in on Sophie.

Everything around her faded, the air growing tight. Pulling him nearer to her. Her green eyes glittered in the low light, her hair shimmering. She was temptation personified, sent to test him. While at the same time reminding him of his fatal weaknesses.

How was it one woman could represent both? How was it one woman could make him want to strive forward doing better, sacrificing himself for the greater good, while also inspiring him to drop it all, so that his arms were free to pull her into them? To bring her up against his body, kiss her, claim her, make her his?

He had no answers, he had nothing other than the burning ache in his gut. Nothing at all.

"Would you mind giving me some privacy while I get ready?" she asked.

He had no choice but to give her privacy. If he were in here while she readied herself for bed he doubted he would be able to control himself.

And with Jasmine so freshly on his mind, it seemed a blasphemy. With Leila, her secret and the weight of his responsibility pressing down upon him, he should be able to think of nothing else. Of Christine and their upcoming marriage.

And yet none of it seemed to matter half as much as what he felt when he looked at Sophie. It *was* a blasphemy. And yet it was one he was not certain he knew how to combat. It was one he was not certain he *wanted* to combat. It was such a foreign feeling, something lost back in time, something that had been bound up and twisted up in tragedy, in disgrace.

He'd had lovers in the years since he'd decided to take his role as sheikh more seriously. But it had been different. It had been with careful calculation and decision. It'd been at appropriate times, and in appropriate places. It had been nothing like this, this heady rush of heat and need that seemed to transcend reality, that seemed to transcend duty.

No, nothing transcended duty.

He could not afford to disrupt what was happening now. He could not throw away his future, his country's future, Leila's future, for the sake of a dalliance with an American journalist who would probably turn the entire thing into a tell-all.

She wouldn't do that.

He gritted his teeth. He did not trust people easily as a rule, not anymore. Not after the betrayal of his friend Damien. And certainly, Sophie was not who he had originally assumed she was. She was not the cold-blooded tabloid leech, but he doubted she was a kitten, either.

She was a woman who had gotten into her position in life with sheer bloody-mindedness and determination. Underestimating that could be fatal. At least in terms of reputation.

Things were far too precarious for him to upset anything.

And he had an agreement with Christine, he had made her promises, and he could not go back on that.

"Of course I will step outside. Let me know when you are ready for me to return."

* * *

Never. I will never be ready for you to return. Sophie kept all of that to herself, but she thought it at full volume. If he could somehow read thoughts it would be extremely helpful. Of course, if he could read thoughts he would know just how affected she was by being in close quarters with him. She didn't like it at all. Not one bit.

She was much more disturbed by him than she could've ever imagined she might be.

She waited until he was gone, then went to the place where the bags were sitting, digging through them until she found a pair of silk pajamas. Of course he had made sure she would have overnight things. Because of course he had known they would end up spending the night out here. Perhaps he had even known they would end up staying in the same tent. Well, he had to have known.

He's not trying to seduce you.

No, of course he wasn't. And anyway, she was not seduceable. Not in the least. Men had tried, and men had failed. It wasn't as though she intended to never have a relationship as long as she lived, it was just there had never been an appropriate time.

She'd watched her mother become a slave to sex, to desire, which she had always called love, but Sophie had doubted that very much.

It was weakness, and she would not be that weak. Would not be that sad and desperate. She'd gone out and made her own life, on her own terms.

Zayn was hot, there was no denying that. He was, in fact, the hottest guy she had ever seen in person. So there was that. And she was ready to admit it. It had been difficult to sort through her feelings for him when she had been half-afraid of him, but she wasn't really afraid of him now. And now that the fog of terror had cleared a bit, she could say objectively that, yes, he was very handsome.

But handsomeness didn't have anything to do with *anything*. She was here to do a job, not get distracted by a pretty face. Though she wouldn't exactly characterize his face as pretty. His cheekbones were enviable, to be certain, and he had amazing eyelashes. If he were a woman he wouldn't need to wear mascara. But that didn't make him pretty. No, he was far too rugged for that. The dark stubble that covered his jaw by midday helped with that. As did the intensity in his dark eyes.

Magnetic. That was a better word for him.

And hot, hot still worked.

She mentally castigated herself while she put her pajamas on, while she tried to ignore just how sensual the fabric felt against her skin. Fabric was not sensual. None of this was.

Annoying was what it was. Well, not the fabric, the fabric was quite nice. But the feelings that he evoked in her were certainly annoying.

He was still stringing her along, too. She didn't feel like she was any closer to getting the scandal than she had been on day one. He was interesting, and yes, she could use the material he was providing her for her career, but it wasn't *why* she was here. It didn't help Isabelle in any way. And neither did thinking about how pretty he was. Or wasn't.

She finished dressing and went to the opening of the tent, pushing the flap back and poking her head outside. It was dark now, the golden light of the sun long since disappearing behind the dunes. Everything was golden brown during the day, fading into a strange yellowish white in the sky, a color she had never seen anywhere else. And now, in the dark, it was similarly monochromatic. Inky blues and slate grays covering the landscape.

She could see he was standing with his back to the tent, an imposing figure, a living shadow in the night.

"I'm ready."

He turned to face her. "I find I am not."

"Oh, well, so then…I guess I just can get in bed now?"

He waved a hand. "Do what you like. I will not be returning for the evening."

"Where are you going?" She shouldn't care, she didn't care. In fact, she should be nothing but relieved that he was leaving. Somehow, though, relief wasn't what she felt. She was just confused. Confused and concerned.

"I am going for a walk, and perhaps I will find somewhere to sleep for the night."

"Well, you can sleep in here," she said, the words dying on her lips when she caught sight of the feral glint in his eye. There was something dangerous there, something she couldn't easily identify. But it called her, tugged at something deep inside of her, made her want to move forward, to close the distance between them rather than turn away. Which was not what she should be feeling. She should want to run, she should want to turn away from whatever that meant. But she didn't.

She took a step toward him.

"Stop," he bit out, the command coming down like a hammer on a nail.

She obeyed, because she was powerless to do anything else.

"The tent is big enough for the both of us. I'm sorry I made a big deal out of it before."

She tried again, even though she was certain she was making a mistake.

"I cannot stay. I would only do something we would both regret later."

And before she could ask him what he meant he began to walk away from her, disappearing into the darkness. As though he had been swallowed up whole, consumed by a blackness that would never give him back.

Still, Sophie stood there and watched. She stood there until her eyes hurt from straining to see into the night. Stood there until she started to feel cold.

She didn't know what it was about this man. She only knew that he was challenging things in her that no one else had ever been able to challenge before.

But what was far more frightening than that was the fact that she wanted him to challenge them. Was the fact that she was more intrigued than afraid?

She shook her head and turned away from the desert, walking back into the tent.

She was only having a moment of temporary insanity. It would pass.

She was in here for this. And anyway, Zayn was promised to another woman. And she would never be the kind of person who ignored something like that. She wasn't going to tread on another woman's territory. Her mother hadn't minded, hadn't cared that her lover had said vows to someone else, and Sophie had seen the destruction it had brought. Sophie would never be a part of something like that.

Though, even if she were that sort of woman, in the end, Zayn would never choose her. Men like him never chose the woman like her. They married the princess, they stayed with the socialite. That was the end of the discussion.

But it was moot because she wasn't going there. She wasn't even tempted.

She ignored the tightening in her stomach that called her a liar, and went to bed.

The next morning when Zayn returned to the tent, he was stiff and cold. It felt like the night air had worked its way into his joints, leaving behind a chill he couldn't shake. Even so, sleeping out on the dunes had been preferable to sharing the space with Sophie. Well, perhaps it had not been preferable in the strictest sense of the word. But it had been necessary.

Though now he was in desperate need of some warmth. For all the brutality of the desert heat during the day, the cold was almost as biting. Though not quite as deadly.

He pushed the flap to the tent back, and strode

inside. He was greeted by a sharp squeak and a flurry of motion.

Sophie was standing just behind the nearly sheer divider next to the bed hurriedly tugging a tunic over her head. A moment later she scrambled from behind the curtain, her cheeks pink, her face void of makeup, her blond hair fuzzy.

"Don't you knock?"

He looked around at the canvas walls. "On what?"

"Oh, ha, ha. You could have at least signaled your presence. You could've shouted, or made some kind of a bird sound."

"If we were staying a few extra days we might work out some kind of system, or code. But as we are leaving, I do not think it matters."

She tucked her hair behind her ears, her expression fierce. "Well, of course you would say that, you weren't the one who got walked in on while you were changing."

"I doubt I would have been as concerned as you are."

"Of course you wouldn't be, I'm tiny. You're invulnerable to me."

It was an odd choice of words, because while he could see her point, he wasn't entirely certain they were true. "But the fact you are vulnerable to me only matters if you think I would take advantage of you. And I would not."

She arched a brow. "So you say."

He gave her a look that he hoped telegraphed disdain. "So you can be confident of."

"Right, well, a woman has to have a sense of self-preservation. The world is a scary place. Men can kidnap you from alleys."

"Is that so?"

"I've heard stories."

He felt a smile tug at the corners of his mouth. "Very terrifying. Are you about ready to go?"

She looked around the room. "I think I have everything all packed."

"Did you sleep well?"

"Quite. The bed was very comfortable. Did you?"

With the stiffness in his joints lingering, and the cold still wrapped around his bones, the idea of a good night's sleep seemed laughable. "Not as such."

"Where did you sleep?"

"I found a comfortable dune."

He did not know why he was being honest with her. He should've told her that he had found a woman who'd been willing to share her sleeping bag. But then, that would imply that he had betrayed Christine, and he did not want her thinking that. Because she might tell someone. And because he did not want her to think he would do such a thing.

The first bit of reasoning was understandable, the second was somewhat beyond him, but it was true nonetheless.

"Please don't tell me you slept outside."

"Okay, then I won't."

"But you're lying, aren't you?" Her green eyes were wide now, the concern in them causing a strange warm feeling to spread outward from the center of his chest.

"Do not waste your tender feelings and large eyes on me. It was nothing I've never done before."

"Well, now I feel bad. Because I made a big deal out of a sharing a tent together and then you went and slept outside."

"You had a right to your privacy."

She huffed. "Yes, of course I have a right to my privacy. But you were going to sleep on the couch. And as you said, you are no danger to me. I do know that."

The warmth from a moment ago caught fire, and turned into something else. Turned into annoyance, and anger. "I would never hurt you, Sophie, on that you can trust me. But I might do something I should not. Something both of us would regret in the end."

"That doesn't make any sense. If you wouldn't hurt me what could you possibly do that we would both regret?"

The flames climbed higher, and he advanced on her. He was beyond thought now, the only thing he could think of was warmth. The warmth she made him feel, that was banishing the cold that had been there only a moment before. And just how much warmer he knew she could make him feel if he but touched her. "Do you not understand?"

"No. I guess I don't."

He reached out and grabbed her arm, tugging her forward. He regretted it the moment he did it, but not enough to release her. "I would not hurt you, little Sophie, I would never do that. No, what I am tempted to do is something that would bring us both pleasure. But in the end I fear it would be something that could cause incredible damage."

Her eyes widened, her pupils expanding in her green eyes, erasing the color. Her lips rounded into a perfect O, and he wondered if they would feel as soft as they looked beneath his own. He wondered what it would feel like to press her curves up against his body, to run his hands down the elegant line of her spine and grip the curve of her bottom. But those were questions that would go unanswered. Because he was determined to turn away from this. Any moment, he would turn away from this.

It didn't matter that his blood was streaking

through his veins like fire, it didn't matter that he was so hard he could barely think straight, it didn't matter that he wanted to taste her more than he wanted his next breath. Because it was something that could simply not happen. Because control was more important than this. Because duty was more important than anything.

Because of Christine. Because of Leila.

Because of Jasmine.

Three women who were all more important than the one who was standing in front of him, and yet, he could not bring himself to let her go.

Which is why you have to. This is insanity.

He released his hold on her and took a step backward, trying to put as much distance between them as possible.

She pushed shaking hands through her hair, and guilt tore at him like a savage beast. "Oh, I guess I get what you meant now."

"There is no need for us to speak of this again."

"But…I mean… You can't just pretend this didn't happen."

"We will. We will both pretend that it didn't happen. Pretend I never said anything." He turned away from her, keeping his eyes on the bland brown walls of the tent. "Now you know why I had to leave."

"Because I tempt you?" The way she said it,

with such innocence, with such wonder, only served to heighten the arousal that was already coursing through him.

"More than anything," he said, his voice rough, almost unrecognizable even to his own ears.

"How is that possible? How can I possibly tempt you to do…anything?"

"You say that as though you have no idea of your appeal."

"I don't. I mean, you're not the first man to ever hit on me, but I don't think I can recall a man ever wanting me when he shouldn't."

He turned back to her. "There is a first time for everything, is there not?"

"I…I suppose so."

He knew that he shouldn't ask her the next question. Knew he should say nothing. And yet, the words burned in his mouth like hot coals. He had to spit them out, or swallow them whole, and leave them to burn him from the inside out. "Do I not tempt you?"

Her head jerked up sharply, her mouth falling open. "Do *you* tempt *me*?"

"I will not repeat myself."

"I would have to be the most foolish woman in the world, or a very classic sufferer of Stockholm syndrome, to be tempted by you."

"And yet, that does not answer the question."

She turned away from him, her shoulders rising and falling sharply with her breath. "Do you know, I've only kissed one man."

"I do not understand where this story is leading." All he knew was that the moment the words had left her lips, the desire that he felt coiling in his stomach had gone unbearably tight, his need ramping up to unendurable proportions.

When she spoke again, her tone was thin, shaky. "It was at a party at university. And he was very popular. One of those very upper-crust-type guys. The kind that I would've done well to align myself with. Anyway, we ended up sitting on the couch together, and at one point during the evening he leaned over and kissed me. It was very disappointing. And yet sort of a relief, too. Because I knew then that I wouldn't feel anything like the madness my mother seems to feel for my father. I knew that I was above it. I knew that it would never be a temptation." She turned back to him, her green eyes fierce now. "But for some reason I've been wondering what it might be like to kiss you from the moment I saw you. I should want to hit you, not kiss you. And yet I find it's just all mixed up. I don't know why."

Her words hit him with the force of a punch. And he gave thanks for the fact that he'd had the good sense to leave last night. Had he not they might have woken up to a world of regret in the morning. As it was, he would take the stiff joints. He refused to even allow his brain to process the full implication of what she was saying, because he knew that way lay further temptation. And he did not think he could handle that.

"You need not worry about it. Because nothing can come of it." He said it is a warning to himself, more than he said it to her. "You can go on as you have done, and I will go on as I have done."

"Of course. Obviously."

"Good," he said.

His stomach tightened, his entire body screaming at him to give in. To chase the feelings that were firing through his blood.

But he could not. It was impossible. Now and always. No matter how much he might want it.

If there was one thing the years had taught him, it was that he desired things that would ruin him. That would ruin other people.

He had no choice but to deny himself.

When they were back at the palace, back in their own quarters, things would be easier. They had to be. Otherwise he would find himself sleeping outside in the cold again, just to try and get a handle on his control.

"All right, then, shall we go?"

She nodded, a determined light in her eye that had nothing to do with going to eat breakfast, he was sure. "Yes, ready."

Sophie could feel the tension stretching between herself and Zayn in the close confines of the SUV. She should never have been so honest with him earlier. He should never have been so honest with her. What had they been thinking?

More to the point, it was disturbing that what had passed between them was honesty.

How could she be attracted to him? How could she have confessed all of her secrets to him, and how could she still want to kiss him? None of it made sense. She knew better than to expose her inexperience, she knew better than to let anyone know when she felt in over her head. And yet she had done just that today when she had confessed to him that she'd only kissed one man, and only once. And then she made matters worse by immediately confessing that she would like to kiss him. It was all bad. All very, very bad.

And it all felt worse now that they were sitting in the close confines of the vehicle, driving down the road that seemed endless, with no sign of civilization anywhere around them. But overhead, the sky was starting to change color.

The pale blue taking on a silver edge as clouds formed, rolling in quickly, looking ominous.

The farther away they got from the dunes, onto harder ground, the worse it became.

"What's happening?" she asked, looking out at the swelling clouds.

"Nothing good."

"Like…not normal not good?"

"Worse," he said, looking out the windshield and up. "It is normal. And I have a feeling I know what's going to happen."

Fear twisted her stomach. "What?"

"Are you familiar with flash floods?"

"What, like on a personal level? No, I can't say that I am."

"I fear we are about to have one. And if we are, then the best thing we can possibly do is pull over and wait it out."

"Is that all we can do?" She was feeling panicky now, and it had nothing to do with their previous conversation. In fact, at this moment, it was all but forgotten.

"We should get to higher ground. Hopefully I can set the tent up before it starts raining."

"You have a tent?"

"Of course. It's important to know how to survive out here, if you're going to go out."

"Well, I guess it's my luck that I went out with the sheikh who happens to be a Boy Scout."

"I don't know about a Boy Scout. But I do know how to keep us alive."

The relief that washed over her was palpable. Silly, because not even a drop of rain had fallen yet, and she was already imagining great torrents of water rushing down the road to meet them. She was being overdramatic again. But then when one was concerned about being washed away on a tide, was there such a thing as being overdramatic?

He maneuvered the vehicle off the road, and she gripped the door handle, trying to brace herself as they rolled over bumps, up an untraveled hillside. "I'm going to keep driving until I feel like we're high enough, okay?"

She was somewhat touched that he seemed to have sensed her nerves, and somewhat defensive also. Because she didn't like people to see her weaknesses, but then hadn't she already showed hers to him? Not now, but earlier. Anyway, she supposed there were no points for pretending she knew what she was doing out here. It was obvious she didn't. She was a stranger in a strange land, so to speak.

The thought made her feel an odd kind of weightlessness, and it had nothing to do with the pitching and rolling of the vehicle. Out here, in this vast, unknown desert, there was no reason to pretend. Because he already knew.

"Okay." They kept on driving until they reached the top of the ridge, and then Zayn put the vehicle in Park.

"We'll make camp here. We may not need to stay, but if it does start to rain it will flood the road. All of it will run down the side of this embankment, and none of it should pool here. We should be safe."

"Your tent is going to keep us dry in a torrential downpour?"

"Of course it will. It isn't as though it's the sort of thing you could buy at a sporting goods store. It is made for this kind of weather."

"I suppose that's the perk of being royalty."

"This has nothing to do with being royalty. Nothing to do with the latest technology. These tents were made by Surhaadi's finest craftsmen. Using the same techniques that have been used for hundreds of years. We have always had rain such as this in the desert, and sandstorms. And we have always needed to seek shelter away from it."

She looked back up at the sky, which had grown even angrier in the past few minutes. "I suppose we should hurry."

"What do you mean 'we'?" He opened the driver side door and got out.

She opened her door, and followed. "Well, I

didn't figure I would leave you to set up the tent all by yourself."

"Do you know how to set up a tent?"

"Not really. Not much camping happening while growing up in suburban New York. But still, I thought you might need help holding some things, or something."

He raised the dark brow. "Or something."

He rounded the SUV and opened the back hatch, pulling out a compact bundle. It didn't look like it could be much of anything, much less large enough for the two of them. But then, she doubted it would be anything half so large or luxurious as the one she had stayed in with the tribe last night.

"Will Jamal and his people be all right?" It occurred to her suddenly that they seemed to be at a lower elevation.

"Yes, that area is not so affected by these thunderstorms. The ground has more moisture and the water sinks faster. Even if they get a downpour it's very likely it won't flood."

"It's amazing how different it can be only fifty miles away."

"Yes, indeed. The capital city is built at a higher elevation so that torrential downpours like this don't affect the infrastructure. Jamal and his tribe stay farther east where they are not as likely to get floods. It's this in-between part that is less hospitable to all."

He picked up the bundle and slung it over his shoulder, walking across the expanse of bare ground to a place on the ridge that seemed to be flat. At least as flat as they were going to find on the rocky terrain.

He started to unpack the bundle.

"Is there anything I can do?"

He looked up at the sky. "Well, if it starts to rain you could always hold an umbrella."

"You're joking, right?"

He leveled his dark gaze on her. "Yes, I am joking."

"I didn't know you could do that."

He smiled, and she felt the impact down to her toes. "I may yet have some surprises in store for you, Sophie Parsons."

As Sophie had guessed, the tent was small. Oh…so small. If the tent back by the oasis had felt crowded with his presence, this would be unendurable. She would melt. She was sure of it. And she could not afford to melt.

But you already are…

She ignored the treacherous thought and went back to examining the tent.

It was not tall enough for either of them to stand. Sophie only had to crouch, but Zayn had to bend at the waist. There was room enough for them to sit, but it was very close quarters and she feared it would drive them both to the edge of madness.

Before this she had had no experience with firsthand lust madness. In fact, she had absolutely fancied herself immune. Now, she was not so cocky.

As soon as Zayn was finished, fat raindrops started to fall on them, and Sophie made a dash for the tent. Zayn followed closely behind, a backpack slung over his shoulder.

"I have food in here," he said as he ducked his head and entered the tent, dropping to his knees near where she was standing, hunched over in the corner.

"Well, I am a fan of food."

The rain started to fall in earnest, as if the skies had cracked open, letting it all pour out now with no restraint, making up for the countless dry days that had come before. It splattered against the roof of the tent, the sound like a handful of pins being dropped on a marble floor.

"It is nothing special." He unzipped the top of the backpack and produced sealed bags of flatbread, grapes and some other fruits she couldn't readily identify.

"It all works."

He also took out two bottles of water, handing her one and keeping one for himself.

He adjusted his position so that he was sitting with his legs crossed and he gestured for her to sit, as well. She did, unscrewing the cap on the water bottle and taking a long drink.

He extended his hand and offered the bag to her. She plucked one round purple fruit off the stem and popped it into her mouth. She suddenly realized she was still looking at him, looking at his dark eyes. She looked away. Her stomach was tight, her heart fluttering.

She was getting distracted again. She did her best to get a grip on herself. But she still felt that strange weightless feeling she'd felt since the moment she'd accepted that she didn't have to pretend just now. It made her want to hold on to the feeling, made her want to hold it close and examine it, not push it down.

Too bad she didn't have a choice. Maybe she needed to get a date when she got back to New York. Stop ignoring this part of herself. Maybe that was the problem. Maybe it wasn't Zayn, but the culmination of twenty-five years of celibacy. She hadn't really intended to leave it that long, but all things considered she'd had a lot of stipulations placed on the whole sleeping with someone thing.

Maybe she needed to stop taking it so seriously. Because this wasn't normal. The strange, intense feeling that was blooming in her chest, spreading down to her stomach, and into her extremities.

No, this could not be normal at all. She'd heard people talk about butterflies, but this was somewhere beyond that. This was beyond anything she'd ever heard about.

But no matter how strong it was, it didn't make it any less impossible.

She looked away from him, desperate to catch her breath, desperate to catch her sanity.

She adjusted one of the blankets he had laid on the floor so that it offered a bit of support for her back. "Since we're here for a while...I think it's time for the third interview."

"Do you?" he asked, his expression growing guarded.

Every so often she had the feeling she was skirting around the edges of something deep. Something real. It made her both curious, and afraid.

Part of her didn't want to know. Didn't want to be the keeper of his secrets.

"Since we've talked about how the country came to be, and how the monarchy came to be. I think it's time to talk about you." She took another sip of water and reached out for the bag of grapes.

"Me?" he asked, and there was no question of whether or not he was guarded now. She could see it happening, watch the depth in his dark eyes recede, replaced by a flatness that terrified her.

But she couldn't back down. Not now. She had to get to the heart of why she was here. And she had a feeling it would never happen until she got to the heart of the man.

He paused for a moment, his eyes fixed behind her. Then he started speaking again. His words slow, monotone.

"It is interesting how time changes things. Surhaadi has been a very wealthy country since before my birth. So far removed from the scattered groups of people living in tents in the desert. This has brought positive change, new developments, the opportunity for good education. And yet, prosperity does not always build the best of characters. This is a story about a flawed character."

His tone was grave, stoic, and she found herself looking at him again, even though she'd just been telling herself to get a grip. "And this is about you?"

"When a man knows from the day of his birth that one day an entire nation will bow at his feet, it affects him. I was told the history of our country, but unfortunately I missed the moral. It was all a very interesting story about battles, about destroying the bad guys. What I did not realize was that it was also about sacrifice. That it was intended to form the way I saw the throne. That it was not enough for a leader to simply have power. It is woven into the fabric of our country that a leader must be willing to sacrifice above all else. But those realities were lost on me. Those stories, those values, were dusty relics in my mind. And everything in life was shiny and new."

He adjusted his position and opened one of the bags that contained a piece of flat bread. He tore off a piece and ate it slowly, as if he was carefully considering his next words. He swallowed and continued. "Nothing was off-limits to me and I set no boundaries for myself. I was the despair of my mother, and I earned my father's disdain. Make no mistake, it was earned. My father was a wise man, serious, and consumed with the idea of honor. And I was a son who had none. I was a son who cared for nothing more than acquiring the latest model of car, or finding the best nightspots throughout Europe. I had a large network of friends who helped me gain access to those places. Who helped me pick up women."

It was jarring to think of him in this way. As a young man consumed by the idea of acquiring more wealth. She had seen nothing of that in him from the moment she met him. His only concern had ever been for his family. His family and his country.

"My father warned me that my behavior would lead to ruin, that it would lead to death. But I didn't care. Because I had never seen evidence of a consequence. Because money and power had spared me from every single one. If we trashed a hotel room, I could more than afford to pay someone to clean it up. If we got into a fender bender, it was easy to throw money at the owner of the other car and make it all go away. When I was through with a lover, all I had to do was give her a trinket and she would be happy again. She would go on her way feeling pleased at her dalliance with a sheikh. Yes, I lived my life consequence-free for a great many years."

She tried to read what he was feeling, tried to understand what he was thinking by looking into his eyes. But there was nothing there. Nothing but an endless black well. "What changed? Because something had to. Otherwise I very much believe you would still be cutting a party swath through Europe." And who wouldn't? She'd never had the luxury of living consequence-free, she'd always had to work harder. Had her life been different, she very likely would have been different to.

"You are not wrong. Something did change. My father was proven right."

"What do you mean?"

He drew in a sharp breath and looked down, his shoulders tightened.

"Zayn," she pressed. "What is it that he said?"

There was nothing but silence in the tent for long moments. Nothing but water on canvas. Then Zayn looked up at her, his eyes dark pits.

"My father said my behavior would end in ruin. He said it would end in death. And it did, Sophie. My actions caused the death of my sister."

CHAPTER SEVEN

SOPHIE COULD ONLY stare at Zayn, his admission settling heavily in the room, like a blanket of dust, covering everything it touched. She didn't want to speak for fear she might disturb it all, for fear she might disrupt it, cloud the air and stop his confession. Interrupt what he was about to say. And yet, she found she could hardly breathe in the silence, waiting for him to continue. Waiting for him to explain.

But he didn't speak. He only sat, his dark eyes fixed on a spot behind her, not the tent wall, somewhere more distant than that. Perhaps somewhere back in the past.

"Zayn?" she asked. Her voice seemed far too loud in the stillness, competing with the rain falling on the tent top. Disturbing the natural order.

He still didn't speak, a sharp breath making his chest pitch, lifting his shoulders. And then he looked back at her, snapping back to the present, as though he had never been gone. But he had been, she knew it as certainly as she was sitting there.

"I am responsible for the death of my younger sister Jasmine." He said the words again as though to affirm them both to himself and to her.

He had mentioned his sister just last night, and yet, at the time nothing had been brought up in her memory. But now... Dimly she thought she might be able to remember a news story about the death of a royal princess somewhere in the world. But it was hard to say what was memory and what was her brain trying to forge a connection between this moment and a moment in her past. Trying to find a way to connect even more deeply than she already had. Which was a mistake, and yet she couldn't stop herself.

"And she was younger?"

"By only a couple of years. Leila, my sister who is still alive, is the baby. Jasmine and I were much closer in age. And we were friends. Often, we got into trouble together. Until I outgrew her, until I started to do things I did not want my sister involved in. Of course, I did not want my younger sister sleeping around and drinking to excess. Those things were fine for me but in my mind off-limits to her. To this day I cannot say what I was thinking. Because I do not understand. I do not understand that man. That man I was sixteen years ago."

"Why have I heard so little about this? It seems as though if there were a real scandal here it would be covered in the news even now."

"Yes, and it would be, if anyone knew the full story."

"Are you sure you want to tell the whole story to me?"

She had to give him a chance to change his mind. A chance to leave it unspoken. To leave her in the dark. But she wanted to push him to tell her, too, because this might be the scandal he'd mentioned. The one she needed to stop the Chatsfields.

Did you ever stop to think who else it could ruin?

No. And she couldn't. This was for Isabelle.

His dark eyes leveled with hers. "I am going to tell you the story. What you do with it after is up to you. You want the scandal, and this is the scandal I can give you."

"The scandal I'm after?" she asked, her throat dry.

"Somehow I doubt it. But does it matter? You're a journalist. And this is the better story. This is the thing you need."

Her throat tightened, her stomach cramping uncomfortably. "Is it about James Chatsfield?"

"No, it is not. The only villain in this story is me. Or perhaps Damien, should you wish to cast him as such. But I don't blame you if you do not wish to speak ill of the dead."

Dimly she thought she should turn on her digital recorder, but she didn't want to interrupt him for anything. Didn't want him to become conscious of her recording his words. It was okay, though, because she wouldn't forget them. No matter what she did with his words after this, she would not forget them.

"I'm listening."

"When you live a lifestyle such as mine you attract a certain sort of person. And it must be acknowledged that I was one of them. I was not above any of those I brought to the family palace. I was a part of them. I was the chief of sinners, in no way above any of their actions, and often leading them. These were the people I brought home. And my sister, who had been my closest friend growing up, was confused as to why I preferred these people over her now. Damien was my partner in crime. The drinking, the womanizing, he was there for all of it. I knew what manner of man he was, and yet, I introduced him to Jasmine."

Again she wanted to say something, wanted to interrupt and offer comfort in some way. Wanted to stop the flow of words from coming out of his mouth, so he wouldn't expose himself in this way. So he wouldn't reveal his secrets to her. Because she wasn't certain she was equal to them, wasn't certain she was worthy of them.

She had no armor in this moment, adrift in a sea, rather than clinging doggedly to the pier and trying to appear as though she was secure.

"She was taken with Damien from the first, but I assumed, in my arrogance, that Damien knew better than to touch her. Still, when I noticed my sister's fascination with him I warned her away. I was not kind. I told her that silly virgins should never even speak to men like that. She asked if that meant she should not speak to me. Of course I said that was different. But I started to wonder if it was. I started to wonder why I was content to be the sort of person I would not allow my sister to associate with. But it was too late."

He continued. "One day I walked into my chambers to find Damien with Jasmine. He had clearly given her alcohol, and possibly another substance, and she was impaired. Laughing, and hanging all over him. And then Damien, my friend, looked at me and told me that she was no longer a silly virgin and asked if it was okay now for her to associate with him." Zayn clenched his jaw, a muscle jumping in his cheek. "I was enraged, Sophie. Were there a weapon in my hand I think I might have destroyed Damien there and then. I told them to go. I told him to get out of my sight, to leave my home and never come back. And Jasmine, in love with him as she was, clung to him and told me she was going with him. And I told her I did not want to see her again. I told her…that she had brought shame onto our family and that she was dead to me. I said…I said terrible things to her."

He pushed his hands through his hair, and lowered his head. "So she left with him. And only an hour later we received word they were in a terrible accident, and that none involved had survived. So you see the reason there was no scandal. No hint of what went on between us. How could there be? It would endanger public opinion of me if word were to get out how I spoke to her at the end. Of course, I never imagined he would drive, not in the state he was in. But I should've known. Because the most disturbing thing about my confrontation with Damien was that it was like looking into a mirror. It was realizing that had the roles been reversed, had he invited me into his home, had his innocent sister showed interest in me, I cannot guarantee I would not have done the same thing he'd done. He didn't love Jasmine. And yet he took her, took her from the palace, took her from this world. And I do not believe I would have done any better. I do not believe I would have acted any more honorably. It destroyed me to lose her. It destroyed me that I introduced her to the man who led her down that path, that I drove her away from the palace and into his car with him. And that was when I knew I had to change."

She tried to swallow, but her throat was dry. "That's why you believe so strongly in duty. That's why you're marrying Christine."

"I trust nothing in myself, which is why I don't depend on what I feel. I simply must do what's right. It's the only thing that matters. It's the only thing that can matter."

"Zayn, surely you have to know that it wasn't your fault. Not really."

"Do you remember what I told you about consequences? I had never in my life faced a consequence before that moment. Before my angry words, before my own selfishness, my own desire to deny my behavior for my sister. Killed her. There was no amount of money, no amount of power, that could bring her back. In that moment I was simply a man, and nothing I had would fix the devastation that I had wrought. It was my consequence. One I could not pay off. One I could not ignore. And I will not turn from it now. A man is meant to learn from his mistakes, to learn from the ramifications of his actions. I'd avoided that for years. Until the moment I could not avoid it anymore. So I bear it now, so I let it change me. Because if not, then her death truly is in vain. That cannot be."

He stood, stooped beneath the roof of the tent, a strange kind of desolation in his dark eyes. "What are you doing?" she asked.

"I am going out to check the SUV. And to get a look at the roads. I will return."

He pushed open the flap on the tent and went out into the downpour, leaving her sitting there, shell-shocked and alone.

And then she realized, this was the end of the story. Or rather the end as it had happened so far. Ultimately, it would end with the wedding, the wedding to Christine. A wedding that was taking place as part of Zayn's quest for atonement. The story of the nation, the story of the monarchy and the story of Zayn. He had told her to try and make her understand why he felt he'd fallen short, why he must go on to do his duty for his people.

And she ached for him, for the pain he had been through when he lost his sister. But she could not blame him. She could not blame him because she had spent her life refusing to accept what she had been given. Refusing to allow the decisions of other people to shape who she was. Jasmine had made a decision, one that might have been different with the benefit of age, but a decision all the same.

When Sophie had been that age she had already decided she would not drink or do drugs. She had already decided that she had too many things ahead of her to allow herself to be distracted. She barely had friends, she'd never dated. Maybe her decisions hadn't been healthier, but she'd been safe. And in many ways, she'd been in control of her fate, rather than someone who'd followed a guy blindly.

She had never seen the point of sitting back and blaming her father, her mother, for her situation in life. Not when she could transcend it.

Jasmine, as tragic as her death was, could have done the same. And may well have if her poor decision had not been the first and last poor decision she'd ever made. Life was unfair that way. There were those who made mistake after mistake and came out just fine, and there were those who put one foot wrong and paid a dear cost.

But Jasmine's hand had not been forced. Not by Zayn, not by anyone.

She burst into a sitting position, and scurried out the door of the tent, shrieking when a fat drop of water landed on her head and rolled down her face. The rain was cold, torrential, creating tributaries that flowed down the side of the embankment, down to the road below. A road that now appeared to be a river.

She looked toward the SUV, but didn't see Zayn anywhere. Then she looked the other way, and saw nothing but scrub brush and dark clouds. "Zayn!" she called, looking all around, hoping to catch sight of him. But she couldn't. She didn't see him anywhere. "Zayn!" She called his name again.

Her voice was swallowed up by the wind, swallowed up by the falling rain.

She pressed forward, moving away from the tent, away from the vehicle. Because she had a feeling he had gone toward the wilderness. Because it just seemed like something he would do. She knew it, as deeply as she knew anything about herself.

In many ways, he seemed to perpetually be wandering the wilderness alone. Standing separate from everyone else, from everything else. From the law, from modern mores, from anything that might interfere with the protection of his country and his family.

A strange realization, followed closely by the realization that she had been doing the same.

Yes, Isabelle was her friend, yes, she had other casual acquaintances. She went into an office every day and worked with people surrounding her. But she was alone. She did not allow people to touch her. Because she was in the wilderness, fighting to survive.

Because she was afraid of revealing weakness, afraid of depending on anyone. Afraid of nearly everything. And so she insulated herself, kept herself separate, so that no one would ever know.

How very strange that the two of them, wandering alone in separate parts of the world, had managed to find each other.

If only she could find him now, in this literal wilderness.

Then she saw him, down on one knee, rain pouring over his back, seeping through his tunic, his head bent low.

"Zayn?" She approached him cautiously, her heart thundering in her temples.

He lifted his head, then straightened slowly. He turned to face her, water drops sliding down his face, a haunted look at his eyes. She blinked back tears, not sure if they had already fallen or not. There was water on her face, but it was very hard to say where it had come from.

They simply looked at each other, an expanse of dirt between them, the rain pouring down on them.

"I wanted to tell you—I needed to tell you—it's not your fault."

He shook his head. "You are hardly going to

undo sixteen years of guilt with a simple phrase. But you must know I appreciate the effort, Sophie."

"The effort isn't enough. I need you to understand it."

"This has nothing to do with your story. I don't see why you would care what I think."

She blinked against the rain. "I care because I don't think you should carry this burden. I don't feel like you should blame yourself like this. You can't live your life for other people."

"Are you any different? Answer me, Sophie, are you any different?"

"I live for myself, Zayn. How can you ask if I'm different?"

"Do you? I don't think you do. You are here because of your friend Isabelle, even if you won't tell me the reasoning. You are questioning me to benefit her. You are afraid to show that you are vulnerable because of what other people might think. You went to university so you can show your father that you were worthy. Yes, Sophie, you do live for other people."

"How dare you use what I shared with you against me?"

"Is it a bad thing, Sophie? Is it a bad thing to live for others? I have lived for myself, and I've never seen anything fruitful come of it. It brought nothing but death and destruction. I will not apologize for living for a higher calling. I am not insulting you by pointing out that you do the same. But I will not allow you to stand there and accuse me of something that you yourself do."

"She made a choice, Zayn." Sophie continued as though he hadn't spoken. Because she didn't want to process what he had said.

Because he cast her in a different role than the one she had placed herself in. It didn't make her sound like a hard worker, like an independent person who had made her own choices. It made her sound like someone who was beholden to the expectations of others. Who had only succeeded because she was afraid of what others might think.

Yes, she knew she worried about what others might think, but it was only because she needed them to think highly of her in order to achieve what she needed to. She was using their approval, she was not dependent on it. And that was an entirely different thing.

"And I made choices that delivered her choice to her. We affect the choices others make, Sophie. Your life is a classic example of that. Your father's actions affected your choices."

"I make my decisions. I have controlled my life. Nothing controls me."

Suddenly he closed the distance between them,

wrapping his arm around her waist and drawing her up hard against his chest. She could feel his heart beating hard against her breast, could feel the sharp rise and fall of his chest as he breathed in deep. "Nothing controls you? How about this, *habibti*. Does this control you? Or are you immune to me?"

She couldn't speak, couldn't breathe. In spite of the cold, in spite of the wet, she felt like she was overheating. Felt as though she might melt into a puddle, and flow down the mountainside along with the rest of the rain.

"Who controls you now?" he asked, his voice rough and soft, sending a shiver through her body.

She looked into his eyes, and she was suddenly hit with a swell of longing that overtook her completely. That nearly made her knees buckle, that made her feel as though if she didn't close this minute distance between them she would die.

She had been in this position once before. With a man's lips hovering near inches from hers, and she had felt nothing. Nothing but vague curiosity. A curiosity that had been satisfied, to a degree that she had never felt the need to experience it again.

And yet, for all the similarities between these two situations, she knew that the end result would be completely different. She knew she was on the verge of something that would be unlike anything she ever experienced before. And she knew she should turn away from it.

Because there was no hope here, no future.

But they were out in the wilderness together. Two travelers who had been alone for so long, finally meeting in one place. And it would never go beyond here. Would never go back to real life, would never be something that had a future. But there was now.

And she didn't have to pretend now, didn't have to act as though she had everything together. Because she had given that up when they'd come up the mountain. Had set it all aside and embraced the freedom in being honest about who she was, and what she knew. Because she had lowered her shield, and made herself vulnerable.

It was already done, so there was no point in pretending now.

Not when he had shared with her his greatest failing. Not when he had stripped himself bare for her.

"Right now? I feel as though *you* control me." They were some of the hardest words she had ever spoken. One of the most difficult admissions she had ever made. "I feel like you've taken my body and made it yours. I don't know who I am. I don't know what I want."

He gripped her chin, tilting her face up so that her eyes met his again. "Liar. You know what you want."

"Does it matter what I want? Does it matter when nothing can come of it?"

"I have been lost in the past for a while now. And I have done nothing but plan for the future. Perhaps for this moment you and I can enjoy the present."

His words echoed in her soul, reverberated through her. Because they were true for her, as well. The past had informed what she wanted for her future, and she had spent very little time actually in the present. She had always been looking ahead, using the things behind her to keep her moving.

But in her life, there had been no now. There had been no moments where she had simply existed.

But in this moment she wanted it. More than anything, she simply wanted now.

"It won't fix anything," she said, her voice small.

"A great many things are unfixable. Are they not?" He shifted position, cupping her face with his hands, sliding his thumbs over her cheekbones, wiping the rain from her face.

"I suppose so. Although, it could be argued that we are just making more problems." She didn't know why she was playing devil's advocate in this, because all she wanted him to do was lean in, touch his lips to hers. And it didn't matter that it was crazy. It didn't matter that this could never become anything. Didn't matter that he had forcibly dragged her to his country. Didn't matter that she had simply been using him to try and help Isabelle. None of it mattered. Because if those things mattered, it meant the rest of the world existed, and she was certain, in this moment, that it did not.

"A great many things could be argued. For one, that I should not touch you for your sake. For another…" He let his sentence trail off, and she allowed it. Because she didn't want to know what he'd been about say. She had an idea, but she didn't want the reminder.

"I'm a lot stronger than I look."

And that was all she said before he dipped his head, pressing his mouth against hers. Their lips were slick with rainwater, and he angled his head, sliding his tongue across her upper lip and her lower lip, sipping the water from her skin. She shook, the decadent contact washing through her like a raging river devastating everything in its path. Reshaping the landscape, uprooting the anchors that had always held her fast.

He kissed the corner of her mouth, then the center, moving to the other corner before going back again. "Kiss me," he said, his lips moving against hers.

She realized then that she was frozen, simply letting herself be washed away on this tide of pleasure, on this wave of need. And while it was a wonderful feeling, she was not the kind of woman to allow herself to drift out to sea.

She would swim against the current.

She wrapped her arms around his neck and pressed herself more firmly against him, parting her lips and allowing him deeper access into her mouth, his tongue sliding against hers. It was like the darkest, smoothest chocolate dessert. Imbued with the kind of richness that made you feel as though you couldn't possibly take another bite, while at the same time making you feel as though you could go on tasting it forever.

That was what kissing Zayn was like. Like too much and not enough, all at once. Like something she needed more of, while needing badly to break away, and take gulps of air.

But she continued to indulge, because he was holding her tight. Because he was so firm and sure. A pillar for her to cling to in the storm.

He was stability, and desire. Strength and heat. And she wanted nothing more than to cling to him until it all subsided. Though now, she could not tell if the greater storm waged above them, or inside of them. Between them.

She squeezed her eyes shut tight and kissed him with all of the ferocity in her body. Because she wanted to, and because she wanted him to know that he was okay. That he was not a terrible man, but a man who was worthy of this moment. Of being the only man she had ever wanted to kiss in this way. She didn't know if her admiration was worth anything, but she would give it to him, if it would only take away that terrible haunted look in his eyes.

When they parted, they were both breathing heavily, both soaked through with rain. "We should get back to the tent," he said.

She didn't want to go back to the tent, because she feared it would break the spell they were under right now, right here. Back in the tent, sanity may return, and she didn't want it to come back. She didn't want reality to intrude at all. She would rather stand in the rain and nearly drown in it than go back where it was dry and warm and lose this connection they had found out here.

He must have sensed her hesitancy, because he traced her upper lip with his thumb, his eyes never leaving hers. "I will not pretend this didn't happen."

She nodded and he moved away from her, walking back in the direction of the tent. She stood for a moment and watched him, before going after him.

She followed him inside, suddenly very aware of the fact that her clothes were sticking to her skin. That she was cold. That she was shivering. She had not anticipated being cold out in the middle of the Surhaadi desert.

Of course, she hadn't anticipated being caught in a downpour, either.

Her teeth chattered, and Zayn looked at her. The concern in his eyes made her warmer. And she wondered when the last time was that she'd been looked at that way. If she ever had been. When last someone had wanted to take care of her. When last she had wanted to let someone.

"You will freeze in that."

She lifted her shoulder. "I suppose I might. It is very cold."

"You could take it off." His voice was rough, and it brushed against her nerves, sending a shower of sparks through her.

She nodded wordlessly, catching the hem of her top and tugging it over her head before she could think twice. For some reason, it did not seem embarrassing. For some reason, it seemed as natural as breathing.

She pushed the linen pants down her legs, and stepped out of them. She was only wearing her underwear now, Zayn's eyes sharp, intense, as he looked her over.

Her hands shook as she reached around behind her and unclasped her bra, discarding it along with the rest of her clothes.

Zayn bent and picked up a blanket, holding it out to her. "Get warm."

It was a command, and one she felt compelled to obey, even though she thought it was strange he wanted her to cover up now that she had uncovered.

She wrapped the blanket around her shoulders, closing it in the front. And then she looked at Zayn, her mouth drying. He had pulled his shirt off, leaving him standing half-naked in front of her, his broad chest and slim waist on display. Every muscle was clearly defined, brushed lightly with the perfect amount of dark body hair. She'd been around half-naked men at pool parties, of course, but for some reason she had never been quite so conscious of all the skin on display. Perhaps because she had not been standing less than a foot away from them completely naked. Perhaps because she had not kissed them.

And perhaps because they hadn't looked at her as though she was dessert and they were starving.

She started trembling again, and this time it wasn't because of the cold.

He turned away from her, and pushed his pants down to the floor, her eyes widening when she saw his backside, the fabric of his dark underwear clinging tightly to his skin. Some mature, sensual part of her recognized that he was a work of art. While a much more prurient side of her nature only registered that he was hot and she wanted to touch him.

Of course, if she did touch him, she would have no idea what to do with him.

Really, she had only just got her first proper kiss a few moments ago. She didn't think she was ready for more. She didn't think she could possibly pull off more.

He turned back to her and she tried to redirect her gaze. "I think we would both be warmer if we laid down."

"Sure." She nodded dumbly, not entirely sure if she'd spoken, or if she had just stared at him like a dazed marmoset, all wide eyes and soaking wet hair.

He went over to the nest of blankets that was in the corner of the tent, and rearranged the pillows. She swallowed hard and went to where he was, sitting down alongside him, her blanket still wrapped firmly around her.

"You know, the quickest way to get warm is to be skin to skin," he said, his tone grave.

She opened up the front of her blanket and adjusted herself, throwing one side over him and drawing herself beneath the same one he was under. Heart pounding she folded herself into his embrace. She rested her cheek on his chest, felt his heart raging against his skin. The hair over his skin was rough, the flesh beneath smooth and hot. She raised her hand and pressed her palm flat against him, reveling in the feel of him. In the differences between their bodies.

This moment should have been surreal, and yet it wasn't. It was too sharp, too all-consuming. She was wholly in this moment with him, completely aware of who he was, who she was and what they were doing.

She lowered her head, resting it in the curve of his neck. He tightened his hold on her, one hand rested between her shoulder blades, the other on her lower back.

His breathing was ragged, fanning over her temple.

"I want…" She didn't know quite what to say, because she didn't know quite what she wanted. She only knew that her heart was raging out of control, that she felt shaky, that she felt needy. And she knew he had the answer. "I want—"

He cut off her words with a kiss, a gentle one, a soft one. This wasn't a claiming, but a tasting. A question.

She slid her hands up his chest, and locked them around his neck, deepening the kiss. She could feel his arousal, hardening beneath her hip. She shifted, bringing his hardness between her thighs.

He moved, bracing his weight on his arms, settling between her legs. His dark eyes bored into hers, his focus unwavering.

"Sophie—" his voice was rough "—do you know what you're asking for?"

Pressure built in her chest, built in her body, squeezing her throat tight. All she could do was nod. And she hoped she was being honest.

This seemed like the right time. It seemed like the right place.

He seemed like the wrong man. Engaged to another woman, the ruler of a country worlds apart from her own. A man who controlled the fate of the nation, a man who held the fate of millions in the palm of his hand.

He seemed like the wrong man, but at the same time he seemed like the only man. Because no one else had come close to this, no one else had made her feel this way.

Attraction, lust, it always seemed like something terrifying to her. Something to be avoided. It had seemed like great bouts of weeping, depression and a stalled-out life that was enslaved by one person who held all the control, all in the name of something that was supposed to be love.

But this wasn't like that at all. This had been so easy. So easy to kiss him. So easy to take her clothes off for him. So easy to lay down with him, and let him take her into his arms. It was right in a way she had never imagined something like this could be.

He pressed a kiss to her shoulder, before lifting his head and looking into her eyes, sweeping her hair out of her face. Yes, when she looked at his face it made it all feel very easy.

She had to wonder at who she was right now, at who this woman, lying in a desert tent in the arms of a man who should feel like a stranger, was. Because a week ago this wouldn't have been possible. A week ago she would never have been able to imagine this.

She didn't know what she was doing, and it was okay. For the first time it was okay. Because she had stripped off her clothes in the tent, but she had stripped off her armor down at the bottom of the mountain. And now she could feel everything. Every touch, every whisper against her skin, unprotected, vulnerable, exposed. But it wasn't scary.

It was right. It was everything.

"Sophie," he said her name again, "I need you to say you want this. I need to know."

"Of course I do, Zayn." She put her hand on his cheek, kept her eyes on his. "How could I not? I think this was always going to happen. From the very first."

Whether it made sense or not, there had been something compelling about him from the instant they'd laid eyes on each other. Something different. Whether it made sense or not, knowing him had begun changing her from that very first moment.

"Nothing is inevitable. Isn't it all about choices? Weren't you just saying that?"

Something shifted inside of her, an avalanche of feelings pouring through her. "Yes, it is about choices. I had a choice when we met. If I had told you I was leaving, you would have let me go. I'm confident in that now. You didn't force me, even if you did manipulate the situation. I chose to come with you. I'm choosing to be here now. I'm choosing this."

"I shouldn't," he said.

Her heart squeezed tight. "I know." Because she did know, she knew that this didn't make sense. But she also knew she needed it. Needed him. "Doesn't it feel like we're the only ones in the world?"

"Out here it's easy to believe," he said.

"Yes, a little bit too easy. But you have to know that I feel different right now. What you said about why I make choices… It was true. Everything I do has been in reaction to other people. But if other people didn't exist, if there was nothing but this, if there weren't kingdoms, and cities. If there weren't mansions and hovels, if there weren't haves and have-nots. If there was only this, I would want to be here with you. And I know that when we leave, all of that other stuff will come back. But right now, right now it's not here."

He closed his eyes, letting his head fall back, his expression pained. Then he lowered his head, opening his eyes slowly, black fire blazing from them. "If there are no kingdoms, then there are no kings. And if there are no kings, there is no duty that must be kept. And if there is no duty, if there is only myself, then I choose you."

She swallowed hard, an ache building in her chest, her throat burning. "Please," she whispered. "Please, choose me."

He groaned and cupped her cheeks, kissing her deeply, his tongue sliding against hers. She wrapped her arms around his neck, opened herself to him. He tangled his fingers through her hair, let one hand slide down the curve of her neck, down her back, before he shifted position and cupped her rear, tugging her up against him. He kept on kissing her, the world beyond the desert a distant memory, and the desert itself slowly falling away, sand through an hourglass. It was a countdown timer that couldn't be denied. But she was also weightless, falling, all while being held in Zayn's arms.

He abandoned her mouth, kissed the hollow of her throat, before moving lower, tracing the valley between her breasts with his tongue before adjusting position and sliding the flat of his tongue over one hardened nipple. She gasped, arching her back, pressing herself more firmly against him.

A dull ache beat at the apex of her thighs, a deep feeling of emptiness at her core. She had no idea being hollow could be painful, but it was. In this moment it was.

He palmed her breast with his other hand, as he drew one tight bud into his mouth. She laced her fingers through his hair and held him tightly against her, not wanting the sensual assault to end.

He lifted his head, and she released her hold on him reluctantly. "Sophie, I need to ask you something."

She shook her head. She knew whatever it was she didn't want to talk about it right now. Because she didn't want to talk about anything right now. She only wanted to feel, she didn't want to think. She didn't want to discuss.

Instead, she hooked her fingers in the waistband of her panties and shoved them down as far as she could, kicking them the rest of the way when she could no longer reach, her eyes locked with his as she did.

He nodded slowly, then he shifted, tugging his own underwear down. Then he bent to kiss her again, his lips soft and tender against hers. A surprise after the claiming from earlier. He shifted his weight, and put his hand between her thighs, guiding his fingertips through her slick folds. She was wet for him, ready for all of this, for everything.

A little shock of nerves went through her when she realized she hadn't even seen him naked. But there would be plenty of time for that, plenty of time later. She ignored the feeling of the sand shifting beneath them, more time running out.

She gasped as he slipped one finger deep inside of her, the invasion strange and foreign. But not unpleasant. Not at all. He moved his thumb over her clitoris in time with the thrust of his finger, winding up the tension that had already been building in her core.

He continued to apply steady pressure, continued to keep the rhythm going, drawing her closer and closer to an abyss she could not see the bottom of. To a point she could not envision. It was all beyond her, beyond her experience.

And she was finding power in that. Power in being at his mercy, power in allowing him to teach her. To show her what her body wanted, what her body was made for. For the first time in her memory she felt like she was simply existing, not striving, not hiding. She felt so gloriously out in the open, so wonderfully exposed. And she had never imagined either of those things could possibly be good. But Zayn made them good. Zayn made them wonderful.

He kissed her, deep and hard, as he intensified the pressure between her thighs. The subtle change was just enough to show her how deep the well was. To drag her all the way to the bottom, holding her under until she couldn't breathe, couldn't think. Couldn't do anything but simply allow the release to wash over her, pleasure overcoming her completely. When she surfaced, she was breathing hard.

"I don't know...I don't want to hurt you." His voice was rough, his breathing ragged.

"You won't," she said, the words meaningless, her lips numb. She didn't know if she was telling the truth, didn't know if it would hurt or not, but it seemed like the right thing to say. It seemed like the thing he needed to hear.

He slid his hand on her back, cupping her butt, and lifting her hips as he positioned the blunt head of his arousal against the slick entrance to her body. He met her eyes as he thrust deep inside of her, a shaft of pain shooting through her.

She gritted her teeth, screwing her eyes shut tight.

"Sophie," he said, his voice gravel. "You said I wouldn't hurt you."

"I was wrong. I'm sorry." Her throat was tight, the words difficult to force through the lump that was forming there.

"Don't apologize to me." His tone was regretful. "I should apologize to you."

"Please don't apologize to me. Please. Let's just... Please."

She was beyond speech, beyond thought. Yes, it had hurt, yes, it still hurt a little bit, but it was also wonderful. She had never felt so connected to anyone in her entire life. For the first time, she felt as though all of the pieces of herself and been swept up and pushed together. Made one. Not only was it impossible to tell where her body began and his ended, it was impossible to be anything but wholly her. Impossible to be false, impossible to be fragmented.

It was right. The most essentially right thing she had ever experienced.

He waited a moment, the tendons in his neck standing out, his jaw clenched tight. She noticed the muscles in his arms were trembling, as he held himself still.

"Zayn." She said his name, and he started to move.

He started with slow, measured strokes, giving her time to adjust to the feeling of fullness, to the feeling of his body inside hers. Gradually, the discomfort began to recede, pleasure started to build.

She rocked against him, chasing the climax that was beginning to build inside of her again. His movements began to fracture, his control fraying, everything becoming harder, more desperate. And she was right there with him. She didn't want slow anymore, she didn't want gentle. She wanted it all. She wanted it fast, she wanted it now.

She clung to his shoulders, met his every thrust, her clitoris making contact with his pelvis, white-hot pleasure streaking through her body with each movement.

She could feel herself starting to slip, starting to head back toward the void. She tightened her hold on him, intent on dragging him down with her. This time, she wouldn't go alone.

"Zayn," she whispered, her lips near his ear. "Zayn, come with me."

He shuddered, his body shaking, the evidence of his loss of control the final ingredient needed to push her over completely. Climax ripped through her, harder this time, more intense than the first. That had only been preparation, it'd only been a primer. It had not prepared her for this. For what it was like to lose control completely, with Zayn. To shake as he did. To be drowning in the swell of pleasure, as he did, too.

When it was over, they clung to each other. She could feel his heart raging against her chest, could see his pulse beating at the base of his neck.

And she heard silence, no more rain, nothing at all.

And she could feel the final bits of sand slipping away.

Time had run out, and the world was encroaching. And she knew that she had been a fool. Because she had imagined that she would walk back into that world unchanged.

But she was changed. Utterly, irrevocably.

She had just made love with Sheikh Zayn Al-Ahmar, and everything inside of her felt new. Felt different. But the world, the monarchy, his engagement, all of the social hierarchy, stood firm. Unmoving, uncaring of everything that had passed between them.

"Zayn?"

He wrapped his arms around her, and pulled her against his chest, reversing their position so that she was partially on top of him. "The roads will still be flooded for a while. You should rest."

And with those words, he turned the hourglass again, granting them an extension on their time out in the wilderness.

CHAPTER EIGHT

By the time the light of dawn broke through the edges of the tent door, Zayn had already been awake for hours. He was holding Sophie in his arms, warm, soft and bare, her skin pressed against his. Satisfaction flowed through his veins like warm honey, but then it hardened, turned bitter, as it mixed with the realization of what he had done.

Sophie did not deserve this. She did not deserve to have her virginity taken in a tent, in the middle of the desert, by a man who would have to ignore her when they returned to real life. She did not deserve to be the conduit by which he expended his frustrations. He had reached a breaking point, and it would've been far better for him to stand out in the rain and let it wash over him until he was numb again. Until he remembered who he was. And what his responsibilities were.

But she had been there, she had been there

saying the things he wanted to hear, offering him the things he wanted most. And she had told him to pretend as though the rest of the world didn't exist, and he had been far too eager to refuse.

And then, rather than distancing himself the moment he realized his mistake, he had pulled her into his arms, granting them an extension. Granting himself an extension.

Were his spot in hell not already well assured, and likely well appointed in preparation for his arrival, a space would certainly be reserved now.

Where was his sense of duty now? Where was the honor in taking advantage of an innocent woman and using her to sate his own lust? There was none. Because while Sophie might have believed she knew what she wanted, she had no real way of knowing. A virgin had no way of knowing the ways sex might affect her emotionally. And he had suspected as much, especially given what she had told him about the kiss. Her one and only kiss, with one man. He had known what that meant, but he had chosen to ignore it. And when he had decided to ask her about it, at the worst moment possible, after turning back was impossible, he had known what her immediate deflection had meant. Still he had ignored it. Because of what he had wanted.

It was his greatest fear realized. That he had not changed at all. That he was still the same selfish, spoiled boy he had always been. The years of adhering to a code of honor could be undone by lust that was just strong enough.

A moment that his selfishness could not transcend.

He sat up, pushing his hands through his hair, looking down at the woman sleeping next to him. She moaned, and rolled over onto her side, drawing her knees up to her chest. She looked so young, so vulnerable. And he felt even more like an ass than he had only a few seconds ago.

He stood, as straight as he could in the tent, and found his pants, which were crumpled on the floor. They were wet, still, and he probably deserved that. He pulled them on quickly, and went outside.

The sun was up now, the sky clear. The roads below looked like they had dried. They had no excuse to linger here. And indeed, they should not. He would only do more damage out here away from reality. He had managed to trick himself, but he would do it no more.

He looked back at the tent and cursed. He would still have to go in there and face her, would still have to see her all rumpled, naked, and deal with all of the heady memories from last night. How wonderful it had felt to be inside of her, to be skin to skin with her.

He went to the SUV and opened the back, pulling out their bags and slamming the tailgate shut. He hefted both bags over his shoulder, and went back to the tent. When he opened the flap, Sophie was stirring, the blankets pulled up over her breasts, her shoulders bare.

She blinked sleepily and scrubbed her eyes with the back of her hand. She was everything fresh and sweet, perfect. Everything he had no right to touch. No right to ruin.

"Good morning." He dropped both bags on the floor of the tent. "The weather is nice, so we should have no difficulty getting back into the city."

She blinked more rapidly, trying to focus on him, squinting at the light that was filtering through the opening of the tent. "Oh." She shifted, holding tightly to the blankets. "It is morning." She looked like she was thinking deeply about something, and it disturbed him. Made something ache in his chest.

"I can wait outside while you get dressed if you like."

She nodded wordlessly and he turned away from her, taking the bag that contained his clothes with him, walking back outside. He took in a deep breath of air. He hadn't realized he'd stopped breathing when he'd seen her. But now his lungs burned. He dressed quickly, out in the open, discarding the damp pants and trading them for a dry pair, and a T-shirt.

He waited a few moments, then went back to the tent, throwing the flap aside. She was dressed in a loose-fitting top and a pair of linen pants, sitting in the nest of blankets they had used as a bed the night before. She was looking at him, the expression on her face expectant, but of what he had no idea. He didn't know what she wanted from him, because the reality of what was possible in the fantasy that had been last night created a gulf between them that was so wide it could not be crossed.

There was no way to bring any of it back with them. There was no way to keep pieces of it, keep it hidden. Keep it going.

It was a clean break here, and there was no other option.

"Are you hungry?" he asked.

She shook her head, looking away from him.

"Then we will leave soon." She didn't rise from where she was nestled in the blankets. "And you will have to be out of the tent, so that I can dismantle it."

"Is it cold outside?" she asked, not looking at him still.

"It is not cold."

She sniffed, drawing her knees up to her chest. "I don't like being cold."

"Well, you will not be cold."

She looked up at him, and stood slowly. "I had better not be." Then she walked past him, her head held high, her chin pointed upward. She looked like a little *sheikha*, all haughty and defensive. And it made him want to kiss her lips until she was no longer pursing them. Until she was soft, until she was pliant and ready for him again. But he had no right to do that. None at all. It should not have happened last night, and it could not happen again.

Sophie held herself together as she waited outside the tent while Zayn took it down. She held herself together on the drive back to the palace. She held herself together until she was safely in the privacy of her own room. And then she wept. Great gasping sobs that seemed to come endlessly. And when she was done, she climbed into bed and pulled the covers up, curling into a ball. She felt miserable. She felt changed.

Last night everything had made sense. It felt so amazing. But when they had come down the mountain she had failed to collect her armor. It was lost somewhere out there in the middle of the desert, and she did not know if she would ever be able to retrieve it.

But it was over now, that much was clear. Zayn had made that clear when he'd gone cold on her this morning. And it was for the best. Because it could not go on. Because they could not go on.

He was marrying another woman.

The thought sent a stab of pain straight through her chest. She should never have touched him. She didn't have the right.

She looked up at the ceiling, tears sliding down toward her temple, disappearing down into her hairline.

Unfortunately, though she knew she'd had no right to touch him, it didn't change the fact that she was afraid she might have fallen in love with him.

She had no idea how that had happened. It had something to do with the fact that he had managed to get beneath her protection, that he was the first person to ever reach beneath all the layers she had built up around herself. He had touched her heart. And once that had happened she never had a chance.

She loved this man who wanted nothing more than to serve those around him. Who had taken a tragedy and allowed it to turn and twist inside of him until it had wrapped itself around him like tree roots until they had taken control over him, worked their way in so deep they couldn't be extracted. Until they had changed who he was, controlled him in every way.

She had worked all of her life for recognition, for validation. While he gave everything in the service of his family, in the service of his country. How could she not be changed by knowing him? How could she not love him?

And yet, she would have to figure out a way not to love him. Because she would be leaving here soon and when she did she would need to leave these feelings behind, too.

No matter how difficult it was.

Sophie successfully avoided Zayn for the next few days. She busied herself writing up an article detailing what she had learned so far about Surhaadi and its culture. She couldn't bring herself to write about his personal tragedy. Couldn't bring herself to write about Zayn at all. Because she had a feeling that every word would bleed with her love for him, and that it would be obvious to anyone who saw it. And while she was exposing herself a bit more lately than she had ever done before, that was a step too far.

Part of her had hoped that Zayn would end the silence between them. That part of her was foolish, and she acknowledged that, but it didn't stop her from wishing he might.

She stood up from her computer and rubbed her fingertips over her forehead, trying to smooth out the lines she was certain were etched there permanently now. No matter how many days, no matter how much distance, between her, Zayn and that tent in the desert, her skin still burned with his touch. Her chest aching with the memory of what it had been like to be joined with him in that way. With what it had been like to feel so close to someone.

She hadn't realized how much of her life she'd spent alone until that moment. Until that moment of perfect togetherness.

If there is only myself, then I choose you.

His words played over and over in her mind, echoed in her heart. Made her hope where there should be none.

Before she realized what she was doing, she had walked over to the door of her bedroom and wandered out into the corridor. As usual, her end of the palace was empty, and only the sound of her footsteps kept her company as she moved down the long hall.

She continued to walk until she reached the entryway, where there were a few staff members still milling around. It was late, and it seemed as though nearly everyone had retired for the evening.

As usual, no one looked at her. She wondered what they really thought of her. Who they really thought she might be. If they had assumed from the beginning that she was Zayn's lover, if they cared either way.

She wasn't entirely certain of what she was doing, only that she needed to find him. Only that she needed to end this separation. They hadn't even seen each other for meals, so skilled was his avoidance. He was always consumed with something very important, something that always took precedence over sitting down with her again.

Because he was avoiding her, too. Which she actually found encouraging.

This love thing was a strange business.

Her stomach tightened as she got closer to Zayn's quarters. Anticipation, nerves, excitement, all vied for top position as she continued to walk through the palace.

When she came to the doors, she paused. Should she knock? Probably. But would he answer? Was he even in his rooms? If not, it was probably locked. That meant she could at least try the handle.

She did, and much to her surprise it gave.

Heart thundering in her throat, she pushed the door open.

The lighting in his study was dim, and her eye was drawn to the brightest thing in the room—the fire, which blazed in the hearth. She was so distracted by that, she missed the dark outline of Zayn sitting in one of the chairs until he moved.

It was a subtle motion, his hand lifting his glass from the side table.

"Oh, I didn't expect to find you here." She stood near the door, not sure if she should stay, or run. Although, since he had seen her already, running seemed a little bit of an overreaction. It wasn't as though he was going to throw her in a dungeon.

"If you didn't expect to find me here, what did you expect to find?" He took a sip of whatever drink he had in his glass, and set it back down on the table.

"Well, I hoped to find you, I just didn't expect to be successful."

"I see." He took another drink. "And why were you looking for me?"

"Because we hadn't seen each other. Because…because I thought we might do another interview." She didn't know that's what she thought until she spoke the words out loud. But the moment she did, she knew it was true.

"I think I've told you all I can." He looked

up at her, his eyes dark, glittering hollows in the firelight.

"I haven't." Her heart was pounding hard, her throat dry.

"Are you suggesting that I interview you?"

"Yes, that's exactly what I'm suggesting."

He was silent for a long time, looking at her, his expression unreadable, shrouded in darkness. Then he finally spoke. "Have a seat."

She obeyed, moving deeper into the room and settling in the armchair across from him. She clasped her hands in her lap, and waited.

"So I'm meant to ask you anything?" he asked, his eyes fixed on hers, unreadable.

"It's your interview." The blood in her veins seemed to have slowed, breathing becoming difficult.

"I have nowhere to sell the story."

"So, then I suppose it's up to you to decide what is most interesting."

"Then I'll start with what interests me most." She braced herself. "Why were you a virgin?"

Her stomach tightened, she might have known that this was the question he would ask. Well, she might have known that had she taken the time to think through where this might be going. The idea had come to her on the spur of the moment and she hadn't really thought it through to the end game.

"See, now I have to think about myself. And it's much easier not to. At least, it's much easier to just keep doing what you've always done and never ask yourself why. But now you're asking me why, and I guess that means I have to know. The easy answer is that I never wanted to be like my mother. That I never wanted to be enslaved to the kind of passion she seemed to be held captive to. But now? Now I think there was something else."

"And what was that something else?"

"You have to get naked to have sex."

He looked her over, his expression inscrutable, but his eyes filled with heat. "You have nothing to be concerned about on that score."

"I'm not just talking about physically. Making love with someone makes you vulnerable. Even without having done it, I knew it. That's what I had seen in my mother that scared me so much. Vulnerability. And when you get stripped down to the point of revealing your vulnerabilities, you can't hide anything. You can't hide who you really are. And it's funny, because I told you about the way I think about finding my dad. About how I've had fantasies about going to that party, and saying all of that stuff to him. And in those fantasies I'm an entirely different person. That's my entire life. Working to become something other than what I was born into. To become the thing that I thought I deserved to be. But that had nothing to do with who I actually am. I've been afraid of exposing who I am, because I've always thought that person might be looked at and found wanting. Because if somebody doesn't like your facade, then you can change it. But if someone doesn't like you…that's much more difficult. I think what I was avoiding was being naked in that sense."

A metallic flavor filled her mouth, something she recognized as panic. Because this was the most terrifying moment of her entire life. The most frightening thing she had ever admitted. That with him she was real, that she was desperately afraid of being found wanting. This was honesty, and it was easy for her to see why she had avoided honesty in the past.

Zayn didn't speak, instead he reached for his glass and took another drink.

Silence filled the room expanding like a living thing, building upon the fear that was pressing on her chest.

He set the glass back down on the table, the click on the hard surface nearly deafening.

"And have you been naked with me?"

It was the question she feared the most, and yet she knew she had no choice but to answer it honestly.

"Yes."

"Have I seen you?"

"Yes." She looked down at her hands, then back up at him. "Have I seen you, Zayn?"

He spread his hands. "I'm not certain what you mean by that. Of course you have seen me."

"I've seen the ruler. I have seen the sheikh. But have I seen the man?" She thought of him, trembling above her as he found his release, the intensity that had passed between them. She felt as though she had seen glimpses of the man, like the sun peeking out from behind the clouds. But a shaft of light shining briefly through the darkness did not make for a clear day.

"The sheikh is the man, the man is the sheikh, et cetera."

"If there were no kingdoms, if there were no kings, who would you be?" she asked, her voice rough as she echoed the words he had spoken to her when he'd held her in his arms.

"It is a question that cannot be answered. For the fact remains that there are kingdoms. And I am the king of one of them. And I must do the right thing by my people."

"And why is this the right thing? Why is marrying a woman you don't love the best thing for your people?"

"The preparations are in full effect. I have given my word. Going back on that could be nothing but detrimental. Leila is… My sister is

going through something. I can't talk about it.
It is not my secret. I failed one sister, Sophie. I
failed to protect Jasmine. I will not fail on that
level, not again. I have hurt too many people to
ever risk it again."

She could sense the desperation in his tone,
read the urgency that ran beneath his words.
And she could hear things that were not spoken.

"You are the strongest man I have ever met.
You give more of yourself with every breath
than I will ever be able to give in my entire life.
I have spent years consumed with the idea of
showing up some man who barely even cares
that I exist. How is that even a life? What have
I ever done for anyone?"

"You are here because of a friend, Sophie.
Don't think I have forgotten that. I don't have
a scandal for you. Not the one you were looking for."

"It isn't about that now. I'll help Isabelle how
I can. But I realize you don't really know anything about the Chatsfields." She had realized
it for a while now, and she could barely bring
herself to be angry about it. Because she had
been doing something for a person she loved,
and he'd been doing the same. But things were
different now, now that she understood him.

Now that he had seen her naked.

"What is it about?" His voice was rough, frayed.

"Right now it just feels like it's about you and me. It feels like…it feels like something I've never experienced before. I feel like a person I've never been brave enough to be before."

"We needed to leave this in the desert." He sounded tortured now, angry almost, but also desperate. And it was that desperation that she clung to. "We cannot do this here."

"Please, just for one more night. Please be the man. Because the man is not the king. I want to see the man."

"Sophie," he said, his voice a growl now, "you don't know what you're asking. The man is better off dead and buried. He is nothing. He is selfish, destructive. He brought death upon his house. And he deserves to remain locked down so deep that he cannot breathe, much less move, much less resurface and destroy anything else."

"No, I don't believe that's true. Because I think the man is wonderful."

He rose, fire blazing in his eyes as he closed the distance between them. He reached down, wrapping his hand around her arm, tugging her up to her feet. "You are a fool."

Perhaps she was, perhaps she was seeing things that didn't exist. Or perhaps she was the only one who saw the truth. Perhaps she simply needed to make him see.

She rose up on her tiptoes, and leaned in, brushing her lips against his. The spark that burned between them quickly ignited, raging out of control the moment they made contact with each other. He tightened his hold on her, wrapping his other arm around her waist and pulling her firmly against him, crushing her breasts against the hard wall of his chest.

She tilted her head, deepening their kiss, her heart pounding out of control. She wanted to do for him what he had done for her, wanted to strip away the layers, strip away the obligation, every outside influence that had managed to wrap itself around him and reveal who he really was beneath it all.

No matter what he said, she knew that he was hiding himself. She knew she had to find him.

Because he had found her. And how could she offer him anything less?

She pulled at his shirt, desperate to have his skin against hers. Desperate to find that moment of clarity she had felt out in the desert. That moment of connection. So perfect, so unlike anything she had ever experienced before. He growled, and deepened the kiss, pushing her back against the wall, her back hitting hard against the stone surface. But she didn't care. It didn't hurt, on the contrary it felt wonderful. To have the intensity that burned inside of her matched in their movements on the outside.

He pulled her shirt over her head, giving himself over to this completely. There was no restraint in him, not now, and it was absolutely perfect. Everything she wanted, everything she needed. She wanted to release the man that he wanted to keep contained. Wanted to set him free.

And she damn well would.

She put her hands on his belt, working the leather through the brass buckle, then moving to the closure of his pants. She pushed them down his lean hips, taking his underwear with them, not even remotely shocked at her boldness. She would have been, only days ago. But not now. She had left her fear behind.

She had left her protection behind, too, and she was revealing herself. Now.

She lowered herself slowly to her knees, wrapping her hand around his hardened length, squeezing him gently. His breath hissed through his teeth, his head falling back, his Adam's apple bobbing. She could tell he was on the edge, could tell that she was close to accomplishing her goal. Because while she might be the one in the submissive position, he was the one who was at her mercy. On her knees before the king, she was about to bring him to his.

She leaned in, flicking her tongue over the head of his erection. She had no preconceived ideas about this act, she had never given it much thought. Yes, the subject had come up in groups of friends at university. But she had often tuned them out. Because it simply hadn't mattered to her, because she had other things on her mind. She would simply sit there, and nod, and giggle at the appropriate moment. All the while her mind would be somewhere else.

Right now, it was certainly in the present. And right now, she knew exactly what she wanted.

"Sophie," he growled, his hand going to her hair, holding her fast. "Be very sure you know what you're doing."

A sense of freedom flooded her, something intense blooming in her chest, spreading outward. A feeling of strength, a feeling of confidence. "I don't know what I'm doing. I've never done this before. I've never even fantasized about doing it before. I'll probably do it wrong. But I want to do this with you." For the first time, she felt completely at ease admitting that she wasn't an expert, she didn't feel the need to stumble through, pretending that she was in her element. She didn't need to be in her element, not when she was with him. She simply needed to be.

"You couldn't possibly do it wrong," he said, his voice rough.

She leaned in, sliding her tongue more confidently now over the head of him. Because he had said she couldn't do it wrong, and now she felt confident in that. Felt free in that. She parted her lips, and took him in deeper, running her tongue along his length, tasting him fully. She squeezed the base of him with her hand, continuing to tease him with her mouth.

He tightened his hold on her hair, tugging hard as she continued her sensual assault. She could feel the layers he'd wrapped himself in starting to fall away. Feel the grip he had on his control loosening, as his grip on her tightened.

He pulled up hard, and she froze. "Stop it, now." She had never heard him sound so close to the edge, and the thrill shot through her, canceling out any discomfort she felt from his hold on her hair.

"Why?" She knew why, and that was the best part.

"Unless you want it to end this way."

Her face got hot, arousal rushing through her. "That might be nice."

"Oh, no, I can make it so much better for you."

He took hold of both of her arms, and lifted her to her feet, before shifting positions, and sweeping her up into his arms. He held her tightly to his chest as he strode through the study, heading deeper into his quarters. She looped her arms around his neck, her eyes fixed on his. But he wasn't looking at her. He was looking ahead.

She leaned in and kissed his neck, pressing her lips right over the place where his pulse throbbed.

He pushed open the door, and she looked away from him so that she could take in their new surroundings. Her breath caught in her throat when she saw the size of the bed at the far end of the room. Being with him had been perfect, even in a pile of blankets, in a tent. This, *this* was a fantasy. A fantasy and a half. One she had never allowed herself, one that she almost ached over not having had before. Because it might have made the moment more poignant. Because it would have been the culmination of a dream, rather than the realization of all the dreams she'd never let herself have. Though this moment needed nothing to be more important. It was impossible for it to be more important. It was everything.

Her heart swelled in her chest as he deposited her on the bed, curling his fingers into the waistband of her pants and taking them down, along with her panties. He positioned himself between her thighs, his dark eyes blazing into hers. "I will take the time to explore you, later."

They both knew there was every chance there would not be a later. But it didn't matter. It made for a lovely fantasy, added to all the fantasies she'd never had before. She might as well have one now. In this moment, she might as well believe that anything was possible. In this moment, she might as well believe in the possibility of everything. She shoved aside all of her practicality, all of her cynicism, and simply embraced this moment.

She nodded. "Later."

He kissed her deeply as he tested the entrance to her body with the blunt head of his arousal, sliding inside of her slowly. She clung to him as he did, as he closed the distance between them. He shifted, gathering her wrists in his hand, and pushing her hands above her head, holding them there, as he continued to kiss her. He flexed his hips, sending a spike of pleasure through her body.

She lost herself in the motions, and the feeling of him inside of her. He broke their kiss, lowering his head and taking one nipple in his mouth, sucking it in deep. He lifted his head as he quickened his movements, as he started to lose himself in his own pleasure. She loved that she could recognize that, that she could feel the control burning away. It was what she wanted, it was what she craved.

He released his hold on her wrists, adjusting his position so that he was holding her hands, his fingers laced through hers, holding them above her head as he continued to thrust deep inside of her. She watched him, watched as the lines of tension in his forehead deepened, before they finally relaxed, as he shook, gave himself up to his orgasm and released his hold on the world. As Surhaadi fell away, as his need to care for everyone but himself fell away.

She watched his face as he became Zayn. Nothing more.

And then she was caught up in the same storm, everything ripped from her as pleasure took over, as she joined with him at the summit, caught in a storm that consumed them both.

She held him close after, listened to him breathe, felt his muscles tremble beneath her fingers.

And with every bit of confidence she had, a confidence that was now placed in herself, in who she really was, and not just in her ability to fool people into thinking she was something they wanted to see, she knew what she wanted. She knew what she needed. She knew how she felt.

"I love you."

CHAPTER NINE

Zayn struggled to catch his breath, the weight of Sophie on his chest suddenly so great he couldn't breathe.

He pulled away from her, rolling out of the bed, cursing himself in every language he knew, cursing his own weakness. He had sworn not to touch her again, and now he had. And now this. A wave of shame washed over him, a sick feeling that slid through his stomach like tar, coating everything it touched.

If it were only him. If he were all that mattered, he would break his engagement. He would keep her forever. But there was Surhaadi. And Christine. And Leila.

And, most of all, Sophie. Who deserved something better. Something other than him.

"Don't do this, Sophie. Please." He didn't know why he was pleading with her, he should have done all this bargaining with himself, he should have done it before he ever touched her, before he ever touched her for the first time. But he had given in so easily, and then he had given in again.

"Don't do what?" She sat up, her green eyes rounded.

"You know exactly what. Don't bring feelings into this. There is no place for them."

"This is the only place for them. I told you, I've spent far too long hiding to start doing it again now." She flung the covers away from her body, revealing her soft pale skin, skin he had just tasted, just touched. Skin he had no right to look upon, a representation of trust he had no right to.

He wished that she would hide again, because looking at her like this was like staring into the sun. Too intense, too bright, a light that was too clean and pure for him to possibly process.

"Are you really going to do this?" she asked.

"Am I going to do what?"

"Are you going to marry her? Are you really going to marry her for your country?"

"Why wouldn't I?" He pressed down hard on the wound in his chest that seemed to be flowing freely, stopped the bleeding. He shut it all down, redirected the walls that she had demolished only moments ago.

"You can't live like this. You can't live your life for everyone else."

"Yes, I can. It's what I should do. It's what I was always meant to do, but it's what I was too cowardly to do when I was a young man. But I do it now, I am determined to continue to do it. And a couple of brief moments of insanity are hardly going to change that. When Christine arrives here, I will confess what I have done. And for every moment hereafter I will be faithful to her. I will be faithful to my country."

"That is no reason to take a wife. It is no reason to pledge fidelity to somebody. Because you want to show faith to your country? What about love?"

"What is love?" he growled, rage rising up inside of him, and he couldn't quite figure out why. Why this was affecting him so deeply. Why did it hurt like he was being stabbed with a pike straight to the heart. "What does it matter, anyway? I've never seen it do any good. I've never seen it help a damn thing. Jasmine loved Damien. Do you suppose Leila loves James Chatsfield? Do you suppose it will do her any good?" He knew he was betraying too much, but he could not hold it back right now, could not stem the tide of anger that was pouring from him.

Dimly, he realized that he was raging against something far bigger than Sophie, that he was pouring it all out onto her petite frame, and yet he could not hold it back.

"What does love have to do with anything? What bearing does it have on the world, on the things I must concern myself with? Love cannot come into it. It is only duty."

"What is duty without love? An obligation. It is empty."

"It's only empty if you don't act on it. I am acting. I am doing what I must."

"Do something for yourself."

"Myself? I do not deserve anything. I had my years of debauchery, of serving me. It is over. And it is for the best."

"Do you know, Zayn? I lived for that moment in my mind, when I would go up to my father and tell him the mistake he made. I directed my entire life for that moment. I stayed in New York because of that moment. Because I was going to claim what had been lost to me. I selected the school I went to for that reason. I worked hard for that reason. I took this job as a journalist for that reason. And suddenly I just…I don't care. I built my entire life around that. Around a triumphant moment in front of a man who doesn't care that I exist. I would give it all up for you. To be here, to stay here. I was going to stand before my father and ask him to choose me now that I was worthy. I'm standing in front of you and I know

I'm not worthy. I'm not a princess, I can't help you. I can't help your country. But I love you. I'm not waiting until I feel like I'm worthy, I'm just asking. Because what's the point of being afraid? What's the point of trying to contort myself into something I'm not even sure I want to be? I can't be a princess, but I can love you. And that's what I'm bringing." She spread her hands wide, totally exposed, totally open. It terrified him to see it. Because she was so unprotected, and he would be the one to take advantage of that. He would be the one to wound her. "This is all I have. But I will give it all to you."

"I cannot accept it." His throat was so tight, it was nearly closed. "I can make no other decision but the one that has already been made. I have promised myself to Christine, and I must keep that promise." It was becoming harder and harder to remember why. But he knew that he must, because it served his country, because it didn't serve himself. Because it would keep eyes on him while Leila figured out what to do with her pregnancy. Those reasons. He knew all of the reasons. And he could not forget them.

She nodded slowly, tears glistening in her green eyes. "Okay."

He reached out and grabbed her arm, pulled her to him. "You are not alone. I swear to you, I will take care of you."

* * *

Sophie looked at Zayn, her heart burning. She knew he was offering everything he could. At least, he was offering what he wasn't afraid to offer. He was clinging to the idea of duty, because duty was important, she knew that. But she knew there were other ways. And she knew that for whatever reason, he was keeping himself from seeing them.

She needed to turn away from him. She needed to leave. But it was impossible. When he was offering to care for her, when he was there, bronzed, strong and naked. Everything she had ever wanted. A fantasy she had never had before. All of him, all of this. She'd had a goal, she had a dream, but it had been so narrow. So limited. Now, suddenly, she saw all of the possibilities, all of the things that she could want, and they were still out of reach. And even though she knew this would end, even though he was promising an end, she knew she wasn't strong enough to leave now. Not while there was still some time.

So she stood, waiting for him to tell her to go. Because until he told her to go, she wasn't going to move.

She breathed a sigh of relief when he closed the distance between them, wrapping his arm around her waist and bringing her into contact with his body. "I will take care of you." His words were intense, steady, a promise she knew he intended to keep. Another duty he was adding to his list. "No matter how far we are from each other, no matter how the years distance us, I will make sure you lack for nothing."

For a moment she simply let his words wash over her, a balm she hadn't realized her soul had needed.

She said nothing, instead she stretched up on her toes and kissed him. She didn't want any more words to pass between them tonight. She simply wanted to be held. She simply wanted to be with him.

He picked her up, and brought her back to bed. And for the rest of the night she thought of nothing but the moment.

When Zayn woke up the next morning to an empty bed, he was certain of two things. Sophie loved him. And he desperately craved that love. He didn't know if he was equal to it. If he could return it in the way she deserved, but there was no limit to how much he wanted it.

So many years of wanting nothing for himself, and now that he did, he could think of little else.

Except for Christine.

Sophie was right. They would make each

other miserable in the end because while they would both fulfill their function, they would never meet their deepest purpose.

Because when Sophie had said she loved him, he'd felt something shift deep inside him. It had changed him.

It had exposed his weaknesses. Brought them out into the light of day. Sophie didn't let him hide. She made him face the truth, face himself. And he knew he could do the same for her.

But not for Christine.

Duty without love is void.

It would be so for both of them. An empty, wasteland of duty, dry as the desert heat.

But for a moment, when Sophie had spoken those words, he had imagined a future that did not stretch out before him, dull, lifeless and bleak. An endless stretch of time that would mean so little. Married to a woman whose face he could scarcely picture. Whose voice he couldn't conjure up. Whose lips he had never tasted, whose body he didn't want. Was he truly going to have children with her? Was he going to bind her to him knowing that all she would ever be was a political means to an end?

Could he truly consign himself and Christine to a lifetime of dry, empty duty?

He had been using Christine all this time. Using her to ensure his stability, using her to ensure the stability of his family. And certainly, she was using him, too, but there had to be more. He suddenly wanted more for them both.

And he knew no matter what, he could not marry her. Not now. Regardless of what happened with Sophie, and he still didn't know what might, he couldn't promise himself to Christine now.

His heart raged as he reached for his phone. His decision was made. It was not in line with his duty. It was not the most honorable.

But it was right.

CHAPTER TEN

SOPHIE WENT BACK to her room the next morning before Zayn woke up. She had no desire to repeat the scene that they'd played out in the tent in the desert. And she figured he would be in much the same mind-set today as he'd been then. Possibly worse. Seeing as she had pronounced her love for him and he had rejected it. Well, he hadn't rejected it entirely, he hadn't sent her away, rather he had offered to take care of her. And in some ways she found that even worse.

Things that had made sense last night now seemed mostly embarrassing in the cold light of day. But then, pride wasn't the most important thing. The fact that she had tried was. Because she had to. Because it had been worth all of the potential humiliation to finally demand that somebody want her for who she was.

She heard her phone vibrating on the table and she crossed the room, catching her boss's name on the screen as she bent down to pick it up. "Hello?"

"Sophie, we haven't spoken in a while."

Probably because she meant less than nothing to him. She was as low on the totem pole as it got, and there was no reason for him to call and check in with her when he had no interest. "I know."

"I hope that things have been going well there. I hope that you have some good buzz about the wedding."

"Oh, yes, great stuff about the wedding." Just thinking about the wedding made her want to shove something sharp beneath her fingernails. "I've had a look at the menu, I've spoken to the coordinator and I even know which designer the bride is wearing. And I may be able to talk my way into getting a sneak peek of the gown. The future *sheikha* hasn't arrived yet, but when she does…"

"There's been a lot of curiosity swirling around the royal family because of this whole shindig."

"Oh, has there?" It stood to reason, it was probably why Zayn's protective instincts were in such overdrive. Though she had a feeling he was just that way all the time.

"Oh, yeah, big-time. In fact, because of that

building interest, I came into the possession of something rather interesting."

The hair on the back of her neck stood up. "What do you have?"

"More than a decade ago one of the princesses died in a terrible accident. It was big news at the time, but you would probably barely remember it. Anyway, the guy she was with was part of a pretty rich family. And apparently they have a recording of the last conversation the sheikh had with his sister. I mean, the alleged last conversation the sheikh had with his sister. We don't really want to invite lawsuits."

She thought of Zayn's pain when he had spoken of Jasmine, when he had spoken of his faults in it. What if they released this tape? What if they resurrected all of that pain, all of that agony he had already gone through, and all of that soul crushing guilt he carried with him every day?

"Yes," she said, her voice wooden, "I am familiar with that. With the tragedy, not with the invitation of lawsuits." Her words sounded distant, as though they were being spoken by a stranger.

"It's pretty juicy stuff. Here, I'll play a little bit for you."

She started to protest, but then she heard

Zayn's voice coming through the receiver. He was shouting, a tone she had never heard him use before. Swearing, words she had never heard him use before. Telling her to go, telling her to get out of his life. Forever.

The audio recording stopped, and so did her heart. Colin, on the other hand, kept talking.

"Where did you get that?" she asked.

"Damien Coltrane's father. Damien was the driver in the accident that killed the princess. It turns out that when his son's body was removed from the wreckage, he had a tape recorder on him. And on that was this little encounter with Al-Ahmar. Coltrane is pretty angry at the sheikh, which shouldn't be too tough to imagine. And he doesn't figure Mr. Al-Ahmar deserves his nuptials to go off without a hitch. Not after Damien's death. Which, of course, Mr. Coltrane feels our sheikh was responsible for. And as you can hear on the tape, it seems like he certainly sent the two of them out in a hurry. Anyway, I think the public is going to eat this up. It'll go nicely with your wedding piece. I'd like for you to incorporate it."

"I don't... No."

"What do you mean no?"

"Exactly what I said. No, I will not incorporate that into my story. It's distasteful. She died. He grieved. He is still grieving. They all are.

That is his last conversation with her, and you just want to play it to create a little bit of public titillation. I don't want any part of that."

"You don't have a choice, Sophie. You have to have a part in it or you won't have a job. Anyway, I need a story. Because it turns out one of our competitors is about to break something huge."

"What?" Her voice was thin, crackling.

"Sheikha Leila Al-Ahmar is pregnant with a royal bastard. No one even knows who the father is. Now if I knew that, I could skip the story about the sheikh. But sadly, all I have is an old audiotape."

Suddenly it all came together, all of the pieces. Why he was so protective of Leila, and why he had been threatening James Chatsfield with an early death in that alley weeks ago. It wasn't only that James had slept with Leila, he had gotten her pregnant. The princess was pregnant with a Chatsfield baby. And that was the scandal. The scandal that Zayn could not give her, the scandal that she needed. For Isabelle… But right now, for Zayn, most of all.

"I know who the father is."

"You do? How?"

"I…I've gotten close with the sheikh. And I know. But it will cost you that audiotape. You don't release it. That's my price. You sell the tape to me in exchange for the name of Leila Al-Ahmar's child's father."

"That's a steep price." He was angry, but he was treading carefully.

"It might be. But trust me, the public will care a whole lot more about this than they will about resurrecting an old accident. This will be nothing but fascinating, you revealing a final argument between the sheikh and his sister is potentially upsetting. You could face backlash. This is relevant, and the news is all about relevance. Unless you're solving some great mystery of the past, an argument that happened sixteen years ago isn't exactly news."

"Fine, you have it. The tape is yours. I'll put it in the mail."

"Promise me. Promise me you won't release the tape, anyway. I'm not that naive."

"You're naive enough to think that my promise would mean much."

"Oh, I'm not. But I'm also not above blackmailing you." She swallowed hard. "I know you're cheating on your wife." She'd heard him order flowers for women with several different names, and she had a feeling most of them were not sources. Sources tended to prefer money over blossoms, as money was a little bit less temporary. "I have no problem letting your wife know about it, and I'm pretty sure she would take you for everything. Seeing as she came into the marriage with a whole lot more money than you, I'm betting that prenup is pretty airtight."

She was playing hardball, and bluffing in addition. She hated the hard edge in her voice, hated what she was having to do. But when you made deals with the devil you had to be aware of that fact. If she was going to give up this information, she had to be certain that it would protect Zayn from harm.

Because the paternity of Leila's child would be revealed. There would be no hiding it forever. Yes, she was bringing it out in the open early, but the moment the story broke James would know that he was the father. He wouldn't need a newspaper to tell him that. The big secret would be out as soon as the sun rose in New York, but she had the last piece, and with that last piece she would protect Zayn.

Because he was already broken. Because he did not need to relive those final ugly words.

"You drive a hard bargain, Sophie. I think I underestimated you. I didn't think you had the balls to make it in this business. Apparently I was wrong."

"I don't really take that as a compliment. But then, I don't really care if you compliment me. All I care about is the tape."

"Yours. We have a deal. Now, you tell me

the name of the Al-Ahmar princess's baby daddy."

"All right, the father of Leila Al-Ahmar's baby is James Chatsfield."

Colin swore. "Now that was worth the price."

"I told you it was. I'm done talking to you now. Make sure I have the tape." She hung up the phone and then turned, freezing when her eyes locked with a very angry dark gaze of Zayn Al-Ahmar.

Her phone slipped from her hand, crashing to the floor, the screen shattering, sending glass in every direction.

He took a step toward her, the glass crunching beneath his shoe. "What have you done?"

It was on the tip of her tongue to tell him, to defend herself. And suddenly, as clear as anything, she knew she couldn't. Because it was better that he thought this. If not, she would continue to be a duty to him, one that lasted into his marriage. And she really would become her mother. A woman who lingered in the background, who shaped her entire life after a man she could never have.

And on the heels of that, she realized she already had been her mother for her whole life. She had judged her mother, thought her pathetic, for staying in one place waiting for her father to come back. Sophie had done exactly the same thing, for the same man. She had simply decided to go to him instead.

But she was done with all of that. She had to ask for better for herself. She had to ask for better for Zayn.

This was part of protecting him. Removing herself from his life completely, so that neither of them would ever be tempted. So that neither of them would linger, ghosts in each other's lives, never able to touch each other, never able to speak to each other. Never able to do anything but ache.

No, this was for the best. It was better to end it now. Better to end it forever.

"That was my boss. I told him who the father of Leila's baby is."

The words ripped through her like a bullet, tearing her insides apart. Twisting them, tearing them, so that nothing could ever be put back like it was.

It was what she needed to do. And she hated it. She had to lie to him, to save them both.

His expression contorted. "How did you know?"

She tried to look neutral, even while her entire world fell down around her. While her body screamed in pain. "I pay attention."

"Why would you do this? Because I didn't cast aside my fiancée and offer to make you a queen? Is that why? Are you punishing me because I would not make you royalty?" He growled. "And after—you vengeful shrew."

She thrust her chin upward, trying to hold back tears, trying to look defiant. "No, that's not it. It's much, much simpler than that," she said, her voice breaking. "A scandal. You promised me a scandal. And you did not deliver."

"The hell I didn't," he growled, advancing on her. "I told you everything."

"But it wasn't the scandal I wanted. I told you, I needed to find out what happened with James Chatsfield. I needed a scandal about the Chatsfields. Well, I found it. And it isn't personal. But I had to do this for Isabelle. I told you, from the beginning."

He turned away from her. "You did."

Her chest broke apart, a flood of pain roaring through her. "Zayn…"

He held up a hand. "Do not speak to me. The only purpose of keeping you here was to prevent that secret from getting out. And it is now too late. I want you out. I do not want to see you again. I will send a servant to help you collect your things, I will send a car for you and I will arrange for your flights back to New York. We will have no need to speak after this."

And with that, he strode from the room, leaving her more alone than she had ever thought possible.

She dropped to her knees, desperately sweeping the glass from her phone screen up with her hands, not quite sure what she thought she would accomplish. There was no fixing it. There was no fixing any of this. It was broken. Broken into too many pieces to ever be reassembled. To ever be healed.

She picked up the phone, stared at the hollow place where it had been lit up, stared at everything she had broken. She hurled it across the room, and broke the rest of it. She leaned forward, her forehead touching the ground, a sob escaping her lips followed by a wrenching cry.

Finally she had wanted everything. Finally she had asked for everything.

And just as she had always feared, it was out of reach to her. Because Zayn could not choose her, Zayn could never choose her.

The bastard child of a rich man who had never wanted her would hardly ever grow up to be a princess.

She had been right all along. Fairy tales simply weren't for girls like her.

And they never would be.

But Isabelle would be protected. In the end, she had accomplished what she had set out to

do. She had brought scandal onto the Chatsfields. She had brought her friend salvation.
And in the process, she had lost her heart.

CHAPTER ELEVEN

ZAYN CALLED HIMSELF a hundred kinds of fool after Sophie left. He poured himself a drink, intent on washing away the pain in his lungs, the pain in his chest. That he feared he would not be able to.

He would have to call Leila, he would have to call his mother. He would have to warn them what was about to happen. And worse, he would have to admit his fault in it. This was his doing, as it had been when Jasmine had died. He did this, he exposed them to these sorts of things, because of who he trusted.

"No." He spoke the words out loud to the room, as if that would make them magically be true. As if it would make Sophie the woman he had believed her to be, and not the woman she had proven herself to be.

He could not believe she had betrayed him. Not really.

She had asked him to want more for himself,

more than a marriage that was simply for his country. She had made him believe he might find that. With her.

This was why he shouldn't want more. Because the moment he did…the moment he did, he ruined everything.

He had brought her into his home, he had given her the tools she needed to destroy them.

But why? He still didn't know why. Didn't know what Isabelle needed, or why Sophie had felt compelled to do this. And he needed answers, dammit. He *needed* them.

He took another drink. And his chest burned, but not from the alcohol.

What was it that she had said to him? That duty without love was empty. Well, his actions had certainly proven empty in the end where she was concerned. And he had thought…he had felt things for her. He had given up so much for her.

And though he wanted to lock her in a dungeon for what she'd done…he could not wholly regret the change in himself.

Yes, Sophie had turned out to be false, but she had also given him hope, hope in something that had turned out to be a lie, but he wondered now what was possible. And he feared it was too late to turn back.

Too late to want less.

"Damn you, Sophie," he said. How could she have done this? Made him believe. Made him love.

And yet…had she really betrayed him? He couldn't imagine it. He couldn't fathom that—the woman he'd held in the tent, the woman he'd kissed in the rain, the woman who'd told him it wasn't his fault. That he was more than the tragedy he'd always blamed on himself.

There was no reason for her to do those things. None at all. And there was a part of him that couldn't believe she'd done it for a story. It wasn't her. It couldn't be.

He picked up his phone and dialed her number. It went straight to voice mail, unsurprising, really, since she was likely to still be flying. He hung up, his mind racing. He had doubts. And he had to know. He had to know for sure.

Colin Fairfax. That was who he needed on the line. Colin Fairfax was responsible for this, and he would answer for it.

He pressed the intercom. "Connect me to Colin Fairfax. *New York Herald.*"

In a few moments, the phone was ringing, and a man answered. "Fairfax."

"I need to speak with you about Sophie," he said.

"Who is this?" Fairfax asked, his voice sounding concerned.

"Do I need an introduction?" Zayn asked. "I should have thought you would expect a call from me."

"Sheikh Al-Ahmar." And now his voice had crossed over into terrified. "I mailed Sophie the tape already. As promised. And whatever she does with it after is not my business. She said she'd destroy it, that's the deal. But she's the person you want to deal with. Not me."

Zayn's mind was racing, trying to piece together what Fairfax was saying, unwilling to look like he wasn't in the know. "What else might Sophie do with it?" he asked, thinking this line of questioning might be best to find out what he needed.

"Sell it to another media company. But I'd sue the hell out of her for it. Anyway, that wasn't what she wanted. She said she wanted the tape destroyed, and in exchange she told me the thing about Leila. But the story about the pregnancy was already broken. It's not slander to fill in the details."

"I don't want to sue you," Zayn growled. "I want to tear your limbs from your body. But it will have to wait."

"Sheikh…"

"You have lost your chance to apologize. Or explain. Be very hopeful that I do not change my mind about acting on my desires."

He hung up the phone, trying to sort through the implications of what Fairfax had just let slip. There was a tape. It pertained to him. Sophie had made a deal so she could destroy it, and that was why she had told him about Leila.

Heart pounding, he stood and was walking out of his study before he even realized what he was doing.

She had not betrayed him. Sophie had not betrayed him. He had known it, deep in his soul he had known it.

But he had sent her away. In a rage. He had said he would not see her again, and with Jasmine, those words had been prophetic.

Terror, anger, pain, gripped his stomach. Echoes from the past tearing through him.

He had to go to her now.

Because he had already lost one person he loved with nothing but venom hanging between them when she'd breathed her last.

He would be damned if that happened again.

She hadn't thought to bargain for her job. Oh, well, you couldn't have everything. Sophie ran across the street, and made it onto the last block that she had to walk to get to her apartment, her arms aching from holding the box that contained all of her possessions. Well, not all of her possessions, just all of the possessions that had been in her desk—her shared desk—at the *Herald.*

Colin was playing hardball. Which, he said, a person like her should appreciate. Too bad she wasn't the kind of person he thought she was. Too bad she was just heartbroken.

She imagined that wedding coverage would start soon. She needed to find a very fluffy blanket to hide under until it all passed. She imagined not even a fluffy blanket would be able to insulate her from that kind of pain. But she couldn't watch Zayn pledge himself to another woman.

Christine would fall in love with him, that was a certainty. Because how could she not?

"But I loved him first." She said the words angrily, defiantly, as she continued to walk down the street.

She was the one who had known he wasn't just stone. She was the one who knew he was flesh and blood. A beating heart.

There was someone standing in front of her building, a tall man, dressed in a suit. She slowed her walk, her eyes pinned to him. His posture was familiar, the way he stood was familiar, everything about him was familiar. But that was impossible. It couldn't be him. He wouldn't be here.

He lifted his head, and his eyes locked with

hers, and even at this distance, she knew. She stopped, and the box slipped from her fingertips, falling to the sidewalk. A little ladybug planter that had been inside popped out the top of the box and landed on its back on the cement. She looked at it for a moment, but only a moment. Then her eyes went back to the man who was now walking toward her.

"Zayn?"

"I need to talk to you."

"I thought you said we were never going to speak again." He had said they wouldn't see each other. He had said they wouldn't speak. Oh, how she had needed him to keep that promise. Because she couldn't look at him again, not without having her heart torn to pieces. And it had already been torn to pieces, barely smashed back together on the flight home, just in the interest of keeping her breathing, and now he was going to destroy it again.

"That was before I realized I had unanswered questions. And I will do what I must to have them all answered."

"I don't think I can answer all of your questions."

"You're going to. I'm going to start now. Who is Isabelle Harrington to you? Why did you need this scandal for her? What was so important that you came from New York to Surhaadi on the promise of a stranger?"

There was no harm in saying so now. Or maybe there was. Or maybe there had never been. She couldn't tell anymore. All she knew was that she was tired, tired of dishonesty. Tired of the dull pain in her chest. Tired of how unfair life was.

"Isabelle was the only person who made friends with me when I went to college. She didn't mind that I was younger, she didn't mind that I had come from nothing, that my family name wasn't important. She got me my job at the *Herald*—I lost that today, by the way—and she needed me."

"Why?"

"Because I made my boss mad."

"No, why did Isabelle need you? Why does it require you to get a scandal attached to the Chatsfield name. Because that's why you did this, isn't it? I need to know."

"Yes, I did it for her. Spencer...Spencer Chatsfield. He's harassing her about buying The Harrington, right out from under her. The hotel is everything to her. And if you knew what Spencer had done to her...Spencer hurt her. Badly. And now he wants to take this from her, too. I swore I wouldn't let it happen. I swore to her I would help her with the tools I had, the tools that she gave to me. My job. You can understand why I needed to do this. Why I would go with you, why I would skulk around in an alley. Because I needed to. Because I owe Isabelle so much."

He nodded gravely, and closed the distance between them, tugging her into his arms and kissing her hard, deep on the mouth. She tangled her fingers in his hair and kissed him back, her foot brushing the ladybug planter to the side as she moved in closer.

When they parted, she blinked, breathing hard. "Why would you do that?"

"A scandal is going to hit the paper today. I am sorry if it adversely affects your friend, but I cannot be sorry if it varies the headline about my sister."

"What have you done, Zayn?"

"I'm going to make an announcement later today that my wedding has been canceled."

"You canceled your wedding? Permanently… or is this just a way for you to protect Leila?"

"It is certainly a pleasant side effect. But I actually called off the wedding some days ago. Just before you left. Before we last spoke."

"What?" she asked, her lips numb, her fingers icy. "You did what?"

"I called off the wedding."

"I'm glad," she said, reaching to pick up the

box from the pavement. Standing up, she stiffened her spine, looking straight ahead, her heart hammering, fingers stiff around the edges of the box. "Because you deserve better than that. You do. You deserve so much more than a loveless marriage. You both do."

"You were right about that," he said, his voice rough. "I was punishing myself, using Christine as…part of that. It was unfair of me. And you were brave. You asked for everything from life. While I was still protecting myself. Still paying penance for the sins of my past. I was going to make everyone else pay with me. I was going to make Christine pay. I was going to bind us both to an unhappy union. I realized that I could not do that. Not to her. Not to me."

"But that doesn't explain why you kissed me. I thought you hated me. For what I had done."

"You did it for a friend. You did it to protect someone you love. Part of me knew it had to be something like this. Because I know you. I know you didn't just do it to hurt me, or to further your career. I know you didn't do it lightly. I knew the woman that I love wouldn't do something like that."

"You…you love me?"

"Yes. In spite of myself. In spite of all this. I do. And it makes me want. It makes me want things I didn't think I ever would. It makes me want more. More than an endless, blank desert of life stretching out before me. It makes me want color. Laughter. It makes me want you."

"I can't believe you ended your engagement for me...I...I..."

"Sophie, I have to tell you...I called Colin Fairfax. He mentioned a trade. A tape. I know you didn't do this simply to get a scandal. I know there was more. And it isn't only because of what he said, but because I knew in my gut, in my heart, that you were the woman I fell for out in the desert. I knew that was truly who you were and I think I would have come for you no matter what."

"Really?"

"I have a bad habit of kidnapping you."

She laughed, a sniffly, watery sound.

"Sophie....what was the tape? I need to know."

She wanted to protect him from this. Didn't want to do anything to destroy the moment, but she owed him honesty. Because she refused to hide herself from him. Refused to hide anything from him.

"I feel like...I do need to tell you this," she said, the words coming out slowly. "Because I want you to know something. Because I want you to understand that as much as I love Isabelle...I wouldn't have told about Leila and James if I didn't have to. Because I love you,

Zayn. I love you more than anything or anyone. I would have chosen you. I would have chosen your family. It's more than just a trade, it's all of that. And since you know about the recording…I need you to know that."

She took a shaky breath and continued. "My boss called after I got back to my room and told me he had a recording. He says he got it from Damien's father. He…he played some of it for me. It's a recording of you. Of your last altercation with Jasmine. He was going to release it, and I offered him a trade. And to ensure he kept his word…I sort of blackmailed him and threatened to tell his wife he's been cheating. Well, and then he fired me. But the thing is, I didn't want you to know about the tape. I don't want you to ever hear it. I didn't want it…I didn't want it out there. Because you have to understand that no matter how sad it is that your last moment with your sister was a bad one, you didn't force her to make the decision she did. We all make our own choices. I made this one. To protect you. And I sort of sacrificed Leila to do it, and I know you never would have. But that was my choice. You. Always you."

Zayn's heart felt full. Like it would burst. Pain, grief and a strange release were rising in him like a tide.

He had come back for her. But this…this was beyond anything he had imagined.

And yes, it brought about the pain of that day. Knowing there was a recording of those angry words spoken between them, a tape he would never need to hear because he could replay it in his mind without error.

"I do not…I do not deserve this," he said. It was all he could say, all he could think.

"You've saved everyone else, why won't you let someone save you?" she asked, the words so innocent, so perfect, he could hardly accept them. Could hardly accept that she was real. That she had seen him, and still wanted him. That she knew his darkest secrets, and still loved him.

"Is that what you have come to do?" he asked. "Save me?"

"You kidnapped me. And I grant you, saving your kidnapper…it's strange. But so are we. I'm…well, I'm the girl from the wrong side of the tracks. And you? You're a sheikh. We don't go together."

Emotion nearly choked him. "Perhaps that is why we are perfect for each other."

"Zayn…are we? Do you want this? Do you want…me?"

"Yes." There was no hesitation, because he had known the answer. Always.

"That's the moment I was waiting for," she

said, her green eyes glittering with tears, "that triumphant moment…it was this all along. I'm Sophie Parsons. You know me. I don't have any money or any status. Or a job. My bank account is empty. But my heart is full. It's full of love for you."

His chest tightened, so much it was painful, his eyes stinging. "I will tell you another story," he said.

"Will you?"

"Yes. Once there was a man who did things for others, so he would not have to look at the pain inside himself. And he met a princess. But he did not love her. And she did not heal him. Then he met a woman, and he loved her with everything in him. And that love is what healed him."

"I hope this story has a happy ending," she said, a tear sliding down her cheek.

"That is up to you."

"This is like a fairy tale, you know. And I never bothered with those, because I always figured they weren't for girls like me. But now… now I think…it was always the girl locked in the tower. Or the girl who scrubbed the floors. Or the one whose father didn't love her. These stories…they're for everyone. They're for me. This is for me. So yes, this will have a happy ending. *We* will have a happy ending."

"You're going to have to be a princess now. *Sheikha*, technically."

"Me?" She blinked. "But…what will that do for your country?"

"Everything," he said. "Because I love you. And a wise woman told me that duty void of love is empty. It is only obligation. And I saw that life, stretched before me. And I hated it. I would have grown bitter. I would have grown hard. But with you by my side? With your children as mine? With love? It is what we need. Without it…without it all, good intentions are dead. I need you, Sophie Parsons, just as you are."

She leaned in, kissing him, tears running down her cheeks. And he could feel her smile against his lips.

"Zayn, you love me. I wouldn't ask for another life. For the first time, I'm so very happy to be me."

* * * * *

If you enjoyed this book,
look out for the next installment of
THE CHATSFIELD:
DELUCCA'S MARRIAGE CONTRACT
by Abby Green
Coming next month.

LARGER-PRINT BOOKS!
GET 2 FREE LARGER-PRINT NOVELS PLUS
2 FREE GIFTS!

⊞ HARLEQUIN®

Romance

From the Heart, For the Heart

YES! Please send me 2 FREE LARGER-PRINT Harlequin® Romance novels and my 2 FREE gifts (gifts are worth about $10). After receiving them, if I don't wish to receive any more books, I can return the shipping statement marked "cancel." If I don't cancel, I will receive 4 brand-new novels every month and be billed just $4.84 per book in the U.S. or $5.24 per book in Canada. That's a savings of at least 19% off the cover price! It's quite a bargain! Shipping and handling is just 50¢ per book in the U.S. and 75¢ per book in Canada.* I understand that accepting the 2 free books and gifts places me under no obligation to buy anything. I can always return a shipment and cancel at any time. Even if I never buy another book, the two free books and gifts are mine to keep forever.

119/319 HDN F43Y

Name	(PLEASE PRINT)	
Address		Apt. #
City	State/Prov.	Zip/Postal Code

Signature (if under 18, a parent or guardian must sign)

Mail to the **Harlequin® Reader Service:**
IN U.S.A.: P.O. Box 1867, Buffalo, NY 14240-1867
IN CANADA: P.O. Box 609, Fort Erie, Ontario L2A 5X3

Want to try two free books from another line?
Call 1-800-873-8635 or visit www.ReaderService.com.

* Terms and prices subject to change without notice. Prices do not include applicable taxes. Sales tax applicable in N.Y. Canadian residents will be charged applicable taxes. Offer not valid in Quebec. This offer is limited to one order per household. Not valid for current subscribers to Harlequin Romance Larger-Print books. All orders subject to credit approval. Credit or debit balances in a customer's account(s) may be offset by any other outstanding balance owed by or to the customer. Please allow 4 to 6 weeks for delivery. Offer available while quantities last.

Your Privacy—The Harlequin® Reader Service is committed to protecting your privacy. Our Privacy Policy is available online at www.ReaderService.com or upon request from the Harlequin Reader Service.

We make a portion of our mailing list available to reputable third parties that offer products we believe may interest you. If you prefer that we not exchange your name with third parties, or if you wish to clarify or modify your communication preferences, please visit us at www.ReaderService.com/consumerschoice or write to us at Harlequin Reader Service Preference Service, P.O. Box 9062, Buffalo, NY 14269. Include your complete name and address.

HRLP13R

LARGER-PRINT BOOKS!
GET 2 FREE LARGER-PRINT NOVELS PLUS
2 FREE GIFTS!

HARLEQUIN

super romance

More Story...More Romance

YES! Please send me 2 FREE LARGER-PRINT Harlequin® Superromance® novels and my 2 FREE gifts (gifts are worth about $10). After receiving them, if I don't wish to receive any more books, I can return the shipping statement marked "cancel." If I don't cancel, I will receive 6 brand-new novels every month and be billed just $5.69 per book in the U.S. or $5.99 per book in Canada. That's a savings of at least 16% off the cover price! It's quite a bargain! Shipping and handling is just 50¢ per book in the U.S. or 75¢ per book in Canada.* I understand that accepting the 2 free books and gifts places me under no obligation to buy anything. I can always return a shipment and cancel at any time. Even if I never buy another book, the two free books and gifts are mine to keep forever.

139/339 HDN F46Y

Name _____ (PLEASE PRINT)

Address _____ Apt. #

City _____ State/Prov. _____ Zip/Postal Code

Signature (if under 18, a parent or guardian must sign)

Mail to the **Harlequin® Reader Service:**
IN U.S.A.: P.O. Box 1867, Buffalo, NY 14240-1867
IN CANADA: P.O. Box 609, Fort Erie, Ontario L2A 5X3

**Are you a current subscriber to Harlequin Superromance books
and want to receive the larger-print edition?
Call 1-800-873-8635 today or visit www.ReaderService.com.**

* Terms and prices subject to change without notice. Prices do not include applicable taxes. Sales tax applicable in N.Y. Canadian residents will be charged applicable taxes. Offer not valid in Quebec. This offer is limited to one order per household. Not valid for current subscribers to Harlequin Superromance Larger-Print books. All orders subject to credit approval. Credit or debit balances in a customer's account(s) may be offset by any other outstanding balance owed by or to the customer. Please allow 4 to 6 weeks for delivery. Offer available while quantities last.

Your Privacy—The Harlequin® Reader Service is committed to protecting your privacy. Our Privacy Policy is available online at www.ReaderService.com or upon request from the Harlequin Reader Service.

We make a portion of our mailing list available to reputable third parties that offer products we believe may interest you. If you prefer that we not exchange your name with third parties, or if you wish to clarify or modify your communication preferences, please visit us at www.ReaderService.com/consumerschoice or write to us at Harlequin Reader Service Preference Service, P.O. Box 9062, Buffalo, NY 14269. Include your complete name and address.

HSRLP13R

ReaderService.com

Manage your account online!

- Review your order history
- Manage your payments
- Update your address

*We've designed
the Harlequin® Reader Service
website just for you.*

Enjoy all the features!

- Reader excerpts from any series
- Respond to mailings and
  special monthly offers
- Discover new series available to you
- Browse the Bonus Bucks catalog
- Share your feedback

Visit us at:
ReaderService.com

RS13